Frank Barrett

Little Lady Linton - A Novel

Vol. II

Frank Barrett

Little Lady Linton - A Novel
Vol. II

ISBN/EAN: 9783337031602

Printed in Europe, USA, Canada, Australia, Japan

Cover: Foto ©Andreas Hilbeck / pixelio.de

More available books at **www.hansebooks.com**

LITTLE LADY LINTON.

A Novel.

BY

FRANK BARRETT,

AUTHOR OF 'FOLLY MORRISON,' 'HONEST DAVIE,' ETC.

IN THREE VOLUMES.
VOL. II.

LONDON:
RICHARD BENTLEY AND SON,
Publishers in Ordinary to Her Majesty the Queen.
1884.

CONTENTS OF VOL. II.

LITTLE LADY LINTON.

CHAPTER I.

THE DIARY.—JOHN BROWN MAKES A DISCLOSURE.

H, if the joy of those first moments when John Brown caught me in his arms had been spread over my whole life, I think I could never have been unhappy! There was more than I could bear then—it seemed to intoxicate me and take away my senses like a too powerful scent. I must have lost consciousness for a few moments, for I remember nothing that happened after he took me in his arms, until I found myself seated beside him on the felled tree, my head upon his breast and his arm around me. I had to think awhile before I knew where I was; and then, with happiness at finding myself there, and perhaps partly through exhaustion, I burst into tears.

'My dear child, Gertie!' he said soothingly. 'It's all right, you know! There's nothing to cry about.'

I shook my head and laughed as I wiped away my tears, feeling how stupid my tears were; but, all the same, I could not help sobbing until my heart grew calmer.

'Come, tell me all about it,' said he. 'There—you're strong again now!' He took his arm from my waist, and, sitting up, not daring to look at him, I sat grinding one hand within the other upon my lap, wondering what I should say.

'I saw you from the carriage as we passed the end of the road,' I began—'Mrs. Gower and I—and I knew you directly; and I would get out, and—and I ran after you with all my might.'

'You didn't wait for Mrs. Gower to run with you, I suppose?'

I shook my head and laughed till I felt as if I should cry again.

'No; she forbade me to leave her. She'll be very angry, I dare say.'

'And why did you come, Gertie? Does the old woman make you miserable? Are you unhappy in the family?'

'No; Mrs. Gower is as kind to me as she is to her daughters; and they are sweet, amiable girls. I couldn't be happier in any family—perhaps no one would treat me better than Mrs. Gower does. I don't deserve to be treated better, because I am not a very good governess.'

'Why, how's that?'

'Oh, in many ways! The girls do things secretly that I ought to correct them for, but I don't; and they say spiteful things about Mrs. Gower and her friends that I rather enjoy to hear. Mr. Gower's just as deceitful as the girls; and I suppose a real good governess would tell all she knew about him, or else give up her situation. That's what I ought to have done at the very beginning, and what I ought to do now, before I lose what little compunction I have to doing wrong.'

'And why have you not done so already, you little sinner?'

'I hadn't the courage.'

'That telegram you sent me made me believe your courage was indomitable.'

'So it seemed to me; but it has somehow grown feeble and more feeble, until at last I could not bear to think of parting with the girls and beginning all over again, with not one friend.'

'Not one? Had I quite slipped out of your memory until you caught sight of me to-day ?'

'Oh, no, no, no! Not for a day, not for an hour, not for a minute, I do think, in all these long, long weeks!'

As I spoke I looked up into his face, and laid my hand upon his arm. He took my hand in his, and, regarding me with an expression of the sweetest tenderness, asked how, in that case, I could think I had no friend in the world but the girls. It was embarrassing to reply to that question, especially with his eyes looking into mine and bewildering me with soft emotion, but he would have me give him an answer.

'Come,' he said, smiling, when we had been silent for some moments, 'you shall account to me for your injustice.'

'What right had I to appeal to you, to think of you in that way?' I asked. 'You were kind to me because you saw how helpless I was, and how likely to get into trouble without your help. You would have done as much for anyone else whose welfare was at stake ; and when you could do no more to help me, you went away quite determined not to see me again. You did not come to see me, you did not write to me! What right had I to think you still thought of me? What right had I to hope for anything, or seek to open again a communication you had closed? What right have I to be here now?' I asked, frightened by the result of my own impulsive action, which now for the first time appeared to me.

'I hold you blameless, Gertie.'

'But you did resolve to see me no more?' I said eagerly, and waited for him to confirm my belief.

He had stripped the silk glove from my hand, and, laying my palm upon the back of his great brown hand, he looked at me in silence, as though he had not noticed what I said. I repeated my words. He lifted my hand to his lips, kissed it, and said :

' Yes, dear.'

His kiss, or that word of endearment, made me giddy with emotion. I know not what hopes swelled in my heart. I was reckless. I said :

' And you determined to see me no more because you saw—saw that '—I could go no further.

' Saw what ?' he asked.

' That I love you,' I murmured; and then, snatching my hand from his, I covered my burning face.

' I saw more than that, Gertie—I saw that I was beginning to love you.'

'And did it end when you left me? Don't you love me now?' I cried, starting to my feet involuntarily, and looking him full in the face.

'By the Lord, I do!' he answered fervently, and, catching me by the waist, he drew me down upon his knee and buried me in his strong arms under his lips.

Suddenly he set me aside, and, rising to his great height, he stretched out his arms, as if to gather strength, and cried:

'Good heavens, what am I doing? Am I a beast?' And then, without turning his face to me, he said quite harshly, 'Get up, Gertie! I must get you over to Marlow somehow!'

He was walking slowly towards the road, with his head bent. I followed, and, overtaking him, I took his hand in mine, and said:

'If you love me, you will not take me to

Marlow ; you will never let me leave you again.'

His face softened at once, and, looking down upon me with pity in his eyes, he said :

' You don't know what you are doing, Gertie.'

' Yes, I do,' said I. ' And I know why you think it is better that we should part ; but you are quite wrong—quite !'

He stopped short, and, looking at me with mingled surprise and curiosity, said:

' What do you know, Gertie?'

' I know that you think I am very childish in certain respects, that my opinions and feelings are unformed, and liable to change greatly.'

' Is that all you know?' he asked, with a little laugh.

' No. You believe that I have a great

respect for society and its conventional customs, and that I could never be content to live away from the old world you dislike, and in the way you prefer; and for that reason you think it better our love should be extinguished, and we should each go separate ways. It is just like my good and brave dear to think that.'

' I am not good, Gertie; and I am weaker than you.'

I took no heed of that protest, which seemed to me ridiculous indeed, but continued:

' Oh, you are wrong to think that of me! I hate London—when you are not with me; and all the people in it seem deceitful, and narrow, and stupid, and unlovable—all except the girls—and their customs and prejudices are wholly disagreeable to me. I would far rather go back to live in Neufbourg, if you liked it, or sail for ever with

you in your ship, or live in such a wood as
this, where we should be quite alone.'

' Or the middle of Sahara ?' he suggested,
so gravely that, not thinking he was in jest,
but only recollecting to have read that the
sunsets were very glorious on the desert, I
replied quite seriously :

' Yes, if you don't think it will be too
dusty for you, dear.'

He burst out laughing ; then, suddenly
checking himself, he said gently :

' There is more of pathos than of humour
in such love as yours. Not many women
now would follow a man to the world's end
blindly. You might marry whomsoever
you chose to smile at with those lovely eyes
of yours, Gertie, and make any stipulations
you pleased.'

' I don't want to marry anyone but you ;
and I don't see how anyone who loves could
make stipulations.'

'Don't you?' He stopped again, and taking my two hands, held me before him, looking into my face earnestly. 'And if I said to you, "Come with me this moment, away and away, beyond the seas, where we shall meet no one who has ever seen us here," you would come without one scruple?'

'Yes; I will be your wife from to-day.'

'But suppose my dislike to conventionalities extends to marriage—what then?'

I could not think he meant me harm. I supposed only that his principles were opposed to going through a religious ceremony which seems inadequate to binding all men and women truthfully to each other. As these conditions passed through my mind, I looked in his eyes; and for the first time they fell before mine.

'I will be your wife,' said I, 'by any form that is pure and good in your sight.'

'Oh, Gertie,' he cried, dropping my hands and moving on once more, 'you undo me by your goodness! I should be a villain indeed otherwise!'

There was a sound of wheels, and over the crest of the hill came a light varnished cart drawn by a fine horse, and driven by a servant in livery. John Brown drew my hand under his arm, and then held up his right hand. The servant at once reined in the horse, and, touching his hat, bent forward.

'I want the cart. Get down.'

The servant obeyed with alacrity, and went to the horse's head.

'Get up, Gertie.'

I stepped up into the cart with his assistance, wondering what was to happen. John Brown got up and took the reins; then he called:

'Matthews!'

' Yes, sir '—the man came to the side of the cart.

' Where were you going ?'

' To Taplow, sir.'

' To fetch something for Lady Linton?'

' Yes, sir. I've the list in my pocket.'

' Give it to me. If *my wife* asks, say that I have it, and will see that she gets what she needs.'

' Yes, Sir Gilbert.'

CHAPTER II.

THE DIARY.—THE TWO ROADS.

THE blow was so unexpected that it took me some time to realize its severity. I had to say to myself again and again, 'This man by my side is not John Brown—not the man I have worshipped in my heart as the bravest, and strongest, and best man in the world! He is Gilbert Linton. He has a wife living; and he has concealed the fact from me, and he has suffered me in my ignorance to embrace him and receive his caresses!' And even then I could not feel that repugnance to him which the circumstances seemed to require of me. I sat by his side in a kind of stupor, looking before me at the road without seeing anything, unconscious of the direction in which we were going ; and, when I presently felt that his eyes were upon me, I looked in his face with a feeling of wonder and incredulity, as though I had been told that he was physically hideous, and that my eyes had deceived me hitherto. It was odd to hear him speak in his usual manner, for, after this revelation, it seemed to me as though he ought to address me in an altered tone, like those wicked men in romances when they throw off the mask of deception.

'Can't quite make it out, Gertie ?' he asked.

I shook my head.

' Rather a rude shock, I'm afraid ; but it was high time you should know the truth ;

and no good could come of beating about
the bush. Better to get an unpleasant
business done quickly than to do it in
a roundabout, breaking - it - gently, old-
womanly sort of way. Heaven knows if
I should have told you, though, if Matthews
hadn't come over the hill in the nick of
time. I am bad or good by impulse. I
might give my own life or take some one
else's on the spur of the moment, whereas I
shouldn't be likely to do either if I took
time to reflect. I've something in common
with the idiot and something in common
with the criminal, but I'm not a cut-and-
dried villain. I'm ripening, though. Once
upon a time I should have felt something
like remorse for the part I have played in
this affair. Now, if the part were to play
again, I believe I should act no better,
unless I took my heart out and put a stone
in its place. I thought in a loose kind of

way that you would find out all about me,
and that, if you met me again, you would
shun me as a thing of evil. That's why I
asked you to tell me what you knew when
you spoke of your dislike to modern society
and conventional customs. It struck me
that perhaps you knew all, and were prepared to redeem me from the debasing and
miserable consequences of my error. But
you did not even suspect that I was
married.'

I felt that he was regarding me attentively.
I shook my head.

'Your old bonne, Mère Lucas, had no
doubt of it,' he continued. 'She was good
enough to say when we parted at Noailles,
that she would not have engaged me had
she not perceived that I was a married man.
It's odd that I escaped detection. Gower
knew all about it, of course; and, if he
didn't tell his daughters, they are sharp

enough, it seems to me, to find out a secret of that kind for themselves. If your opinion of me differs ever so widely from theirs, something in your description of me must have suggested a suspicion of my identity.'

I had not spoken of him to them. The fact that Sir Gilbert was married had made it impossible for me to recognise a likeness to the man I loved in the portrait they drew of their brother-in-law. The only thing which might have prompted me to suspect the truth was his voluntary separation from me; but I was too ignorant to guess at the real significance of that act. Having an instinctive feeling that it was in the highest degree wicked for a married man to love anyone but his wife, how could I believe that the man I loved, and who I thought loved me, was married? These thoughts were in my mind; but I could say nothing, for I felt a sickness at my heart, and, like one who is ill, I wished to bury my face in my hands and get through my suffering in silence.

'You like the girls, Gertie?' he continued, not waiting for me to explain when he saw how troubled I was, but, as I think, hastening to turn my thoughts from the subject he had been compelled to allude to. 'I thought you would. They are good girls—amiable, generous, and honest at heart, I believe—the best girls I know; and they would be better if they weren't compelled to be deceitful and to seek their amusement in the kitchen. Gower's to blame; he ought to make a stand for them, and put an end to that old harridan's rule. I suppose all weak people ought to be whipped, though how, having no courage, they are to be courageous, passes my comprehension. Whipping, moreover, doesn't make weak people strong. I suppose you have little to fear from the influence of that woman; and yet, if you had any friends to go to——'

He did not complete the sentence, but drove on, seemingly absorbed in thought, until we came to a point where the roads crossed; and there he stopped the horse, and, turning to me, said in a low voice:

' Gertie, which road shall we take?'

He pointed with his whip to a finger-post with two arms; on one was written ' To Maidenhead,' on the other ' To Great Marlow.' I looked up at him, wondering what he meant.

' It has occurred to me,' said he, ' that, after what has happened to-day, Mrs. Gower will think that you are not a proper person to be entrusted with the education of her daughters. No explanation of mine will help you. She is quite capable of shutting the door in our faces when we ask for admittance to her house. That road there

leads to homelessness and the loss of every
friend you have. The other takes us to
Maidenhead ; from there we can get to
London, and from London to the sea, to
Neufbourg, to the world's end, leaving all
that is wearisome and miserable behind us.'

'We !' I said, my lips trembling as I
spoke.

'Yes, you who love me and I who love
you. Do you think I should care to make
the journey alone ? Do you think I should
find happiness in Paradise without you, or
be content there, not having you within my
reach, not hearing your voice respond when
I called ? Do you want me to tell you in set
words that I love you with all my soul, and
describe all the emotions that have agitated
me since we parted in that hotel ? Will
you have me confess how it tormented me
to think that you might forget me, that,
whilst I cursed the fate that separated us,

you were smiling at the change of fortune—
how I grew sick with envy and jealousy
merely to think that another man might
win your love? Don't you believe I love
you? Answer me!' he said passionately.

' Yes,' I replied.

' And you love me?' he asked, in a calmer
tone.

' I have told you so.'

' Then why on earth should we part?
You have no friends to consider, nor I—not
one in all the world!'

' You have a wife.'

' What of that? She does not love me;
she never did. A thousand times she told
me so while the fact had power to sting
me. She married me for position. Her
strongest desire is that accident or illness
may put an end to my life soon, that she
may enjoy the unrestricted use of the little
I should leave her. She does not expect

much—a few hundreds that she may draw
at settled intervals is all that her mother
dares to suggest as the proper provision I
should make. Do you think she will
regret losing me if I leave her all my
fortune? We shan't want much, Gertie—
just enough for clothing and food, and
spare rigging and spars for the *Tub*—
that's all we need to set aside; the rest
may go to Lady Linton—all. And, since
it will be a positive advantage to· her to
get rid of me, I have only your happiness
to consider. What do you say, Gertie?
Will you be happier with me or without
me?'

'No, no!' was all I could say.

'That is no answer, you poor frightened
little bird! Have no fear, dear! I'm not
in 'Ercles vein now. If I were, I should
give the mare a cut that would put an
end to this debate. I want you to tell

me which of those roads you will take.'

'No, no!' I said again, clasping my hands to stop their trembling.

He knew what I meant. He knew that I was answering the spirit within me which was tempting me to yield in opposition to my conscience. He dropped his body forward with a sigh, and, his elbow resting on his knee, he looked up into my face with the kindest and most beautiful expression in his eyes.

'Why not?' he asked, after a little space.

'I do not know,' I replied.

'The law is on my side. I can be legally separated from my wife if I choose, and that leaves only the question of sentiment to be considered. Do you see anything binding in a contract that has been broken again and again by one of the

contracting parties? Do you see anything
sacred in a mutual vow made between a
liar and a fool—the liar intending to
deceive the fool, the fool putting his whole
trust in the liar?'

'I cannot reason,' I answered. 'I only
know that my conscience tells me to
refuse.'

'You can reason, Gertie; you are not a
fool. If your conscience cannot show why
it is wrong to be my real wife, why should
you trust it? Reason is greater than
prejudice; and you are swayed by prejudice
alone—a false conclusion drawn from the
false arguments of others. You are fearful
of what people will think, of the aspect in
which conventional minds will view this
departure from conventional forms. But
we shall be independent of the world—we
shall live for ourselves. What then have
you to fear?'

'I fear nothing,' said I, 'but the loss of my own respect and yours.'

He looked at me in silence for a minute; then, drawing a long breath, he straightened himself in his seat, and, taking the whip, drew it slowly across the horse's neck, from one side to the other, reflecting perhaps on what I had said; while I, sitting with my head bent and my hands clasped in my lap, wondered almost apathetically how all this was to end. If, looking upon me as a weak little fool, he forced me to go his way, or if, doubting his own conclusions, he suffered me to go mine, the result was terrible to think of.

'Good heavens, what is to become of you?' he said. 'If we separate now, it must be for ever. It would be worse than foolish to hang about, playing the part of a platonic friend. Yet it seems infamous to leave you alone. Fancy setting a child

upon the brink of a precipice to find its
way to safety!'

'I am not a child.'

'In one way you are not. You must
suffer only as women and men can suffer
who have loved and love. It is hard
enough for a man, toughened by time and
some experience of solitude and misery, to
suffer in that way; but you, a girl little
used to hardship, a stranger to misfortune
—how will you bear such pain without
friend, or help, or hope, and with nothing
to break the dull monotony of your
drudging life? Oh, it's impossible! Come!'

'No, no!' I sobbed; for, listening to
him, I had begun to pity myself; and yet,
while I thought of all I must endure, my
wish to do right remained firm within me.

'Think of the days and weeks and
months and years of freedom and happiness
that a word from you may command! I

have seen you happy—let me see you happy again!'

I thought of the days we had been together and the happiness I had felt—the fullest and deepest that ever I have felt or shall feel ; and in a moment all the scenes seemed to come before my eyes like the scenes in a dream, distinct and yet mingled ; and a sort of reckless desperation came in my heart and sent the blood throbbing against my temples and singing in my ears ; and, lifting my face from my hands, I looked at him, saying to myself, 'Why should I not yield and make him happy ? Why should I be obstinate to make my own life wretched as well as his ? What if it were wrong, and I had to suffer for it—would not my happiness be still well bought ?' But suddenly, as I thought of what would happen if I yielded, a great feeling of shame came upon me, so that I could not

look any longer in his face; and a black
veil seemed to be drawn before my eyes,
shutting out all that had been bright
and beautiful to my eyes; and, though
I know not how, I found strength to
cry:

'Oh, help me—help me to do right!'

'Hold tight, Gertie!' he cried; and then,
pulling the reins up tight, he gave the mare
a cut that made her start forwards in the
shafts. She reared up a little under the
tight rein, trying to shake her head free,
backed, turned towards Marlow, and the
next moment was speeding along the
road my conscience alone had bidden me
take.

'Corrupting a pure young soul—doing
one's utmost to set aside the scruples of an
innocent and loving girl!' he said sombrely.
'A man must be pretty base to do that,
Gertie. Yes, I certainly am ripening.

You've chosen well to have nothing to do with me. The Lord knows what I may become!'

'You will never become anything that isn't good and generous!' I exclaimed, brushing away my tears and resolving to cry no more. 'If that was wrong which you offered to do, it was offered for my sake. Nothing but love could make that sacrifice. You saw no other way than that of saving me from greater misfortunes even than this. And you invented excuses that I might think it was only I who had scruples to overcome and principles to sacrifice. Oh, I see it all quite clearly now! And I am thankful that · Heaven gave me strength to resist temptation; for you must have loved me less had I yielded! And I would sooner—oh, far sooner!—die than that. Should I ever have ceased to reproach myself if I had laid that burden

on your conscience? Oh, we could never
have been happy."

'Perhaps not. With that sensitive soul
of yours, Gertie, you might be very easy or
very difficult to please. I doubt, though, if
unhappiness would have arisen from my
fine feeling on the subject. You give me
credit for motives which never entered my
head.'

'Of course you didn't say to yourself,
" Now I'll be generous, and do this ; now
it will be considerate to say that." We
don't do good things in that way—that is,
when we're really good, and our actions
spring from the heart.'

'You'll do better to think of me in the
other way, Gertie. You can look on me at
least as a possibly bad man ; for we can do
bad things without premeditation as easily
as good—more so, perhaps.'

'Do you believe I can ever think that

of you, or that I could love you less by saying you are not worth loving? It's just because you are noble, and because I do love you, that I can bear better to part from you than to be your—your slave.'

'Think the best of me, then, if it will give you courage.'

'It does give me heart to think that I have done right, even though I did it with difficulty, for surely I shall never again have greater need of strength. Oh, I am not afraid! Mr. Gower will tell you, perhaps—if Mrs. Gower lets me stay—that I am cheerful and—and a b-b-brave girl.'

My tears would flow again; and knowing that, with my heart in such a tumult, it was useless to try and stop them, I leaned back so that he shouldn't see me more than he could help, and had a good long cry. He took no notice, but, bending forward, rested his elbows on his knees, letting the reins lie loose on the horse's back. And so we went on, both in perfect silence, except for the choking in my throat, which I took care to smother as well as I could, until we came within sight of Marlow Bridge. Then having, as I hoped, exhausted the fountain of my tears, I gave my eyes a final rub, and putting away my handkerchief, said:

'If you'll stop, I'll get down here.'

'What for?' he asked, without turning his head.

'That's Marlow Bridge; and Mrs. Gower lives only a little way from it on the other side. I can walk there in five minutes.'

'Oh, rubbish! You don't suppose I'm going to let you go like that! I shall go and make matters clear to that old woman. If she is unreasonable, I'll see that you are safely housed somewhere else.'

'No,' I said; 'I would much rather go alone. I don't want her to know anything about this; and, if she is unreasonable, I can take care of myself. I know the way to the station, and shall be able to travel to London now without—alone.'

'You're right, Gertie,' he said, pulling up the horse. 'You'll find in yourself a better guide than you've found in me.'

He got down from the cart when it came to a standstill. He had kept his back to me from the time I had begun to cry; and now, as he took my hands to help me down, I saw his face for the first time. There were wet channels upon his tanned face, and his eyes were swollen and full of tears. He laughed a little at my surprise, for never before had I seen a strong man so moved; and then he seemed as if he would say something; but, though his lips moved, no sound came from them; and so he grasped my hands as I stood before him, and neither of us could say good-bye. Then the gathered tears dropped from his eyes and fell upon his brown beard, and, with a little nod and smile, he turned away, and I saw no more, but walked away towards the bridge.

CHAPTER III.

THE DIARY.—GERTIE GOES TO LONDON, AND WHAT HAPPENED TO HER THERE.

HAVE tried to set down all that passed between him and me faithfully and fully, with the hope that, having exhausted the subject, I may be able to give my thoughts to other matters, and regain that composure without which I cannot hope to improve upon my present condition. I may not have written all that was said on his side or mine, and in certain passages I can only imagine what I said by recollecting how I felt and thought at the time. Now I will turn to what followed our parting.

I must have looked a wobegone and wretched creature indeed. As I passed over the bridge some children caught sight of my face, and followed me as if I were a kind of show; and the servant who opened the door looked at me with a sort of awe, and gave me Mrs. Gower's message in a subdued tone of voice, as though she had seen me for the first time in her life. I was to go into the breakfast-room and wait for Mrs. Gower to come to me before I took off my things. The house was as silent as a deserted chapel; evidently the girls had not come home from their excursion. Presently the door of the room opened, and Mrs. Gower entered as stiff and stately as the rustling silk she wore.

'Have the goodness, Miss Graham,' said she, when she had closed the door, 'to explain as clearly as possible the meaning of your most astonishing behaviour this afternoon.'

' There is nothing to explain,' I said.

'What ! Nothing to explain when a young person outrages decency by violently insisting upon rushing after a man contrary to the expressed desire of her employer— nothing to explain?'

' No, I could not state more clearly what I did than you have ; and I have only to add that I'm very sorry my violent haste gave you offence. You see, it couldn't be helped.'

Mrs. Gower repeated my words in a tone of indignant astonishment.

' He was at some distance when I first caught sight of him,' I continued ; ' and the only chance of overtaking him was by losing no time. Indeed, I might have missed him even then, if he had not sat down to light his pipe.'

'Light his pipe!' echoed Mrs. Gower, in a tone of disgust. I assented, and, having nothing further to tell, waited for her to speak. 'And pray who is this — this fellow?'

'I cannot tell you who he is—only I don't think he's a "fellow."'

'Can't tell me? Do you mean to say that you absolutely pursue a man whose name you do not know?'

'I didn't say that. I said I could not tell you.'

'Do you mean to be impudent, Miss Graham, to me?'

'Nothing is farther from my intention. On the contrary, I feel that my conduct must have seemed to you rude and un- warrantable, and I wish you to pardon me.'

'There can be no doubt about that; but, before I can think of forgiving you, I must know the name of this man, your relation

with him, and have a full account of everything that has taken place since you left
me.'

'I am sorry that I cannot gratify your
curiosity in any one of these particulars,' I
began, when she interrupted me.

'Curiosity, miss ! Do you suppose that
a lady inquires into the conduct of her
servant from motives of curiosity ?'

'I cannot say. It does not much matter
from what motives you make your inquiries
in this case. If I cannot answer them, and
you will not forgive me unless I do, there is
an end of the matter,' I said.

I had no wish to affront Mrs. Gower;
yet it seemed that I could not reply to any
question she put without giving offence.
Being so weary and dispirited, I was unable
to choose my words, and, seeing that, however I replied, the result must be the same,
I only desired to bring the fruitless and

irritating discussion to an end as quickly as possible.

'Your impudence passes all bounds!' she exclaimed. 'An end of the matter indeed! You cannot imagine that I shall permit you to stay under the same roof a single night with my daughters whilst your character for morality is open to suspicion!'

It was now my turn to echo her words. What did she mean by my character for morality being open to suspicion?

'I am not to be deceived by the pretence of ignorance, Miss Graham. Your appearance is in itself sufficient to justify the severest conclusions!'

I glanced hurriedly in the glass. My face was disfigured with crying; but what damaging conclusions the harshest judge could draw from these signs of grief I could not divine.

'I do not understand you,' I said.

She made me understand her by an insinuation so shameful, so foreign to anything in my mind, that for a moment I was powerless to reply; then, burning with indignation, I replied in passionate anger, and with a vehemence that made her shrink before me.

My face burns with shame, my hand trembles as I recall what passed. Why should I continue? Why attempt to recollect precisely that which I only wish to forget? I will have done with it in few words. My indignation absolutely frightened Mrs. Gower. She attempted to conciliate me; but, had she begged my pardon, I would have refused to give it. She kept repeating, 'You are unreasonable, Miss Graham.' Perhaps I was. I felt like a fury, and needed but a word or gesture of provocation to avenge with violence the injury I had received. I think she saw this,

for she prudently drew back as I made for
the door, and made no attempt to restrain
me from going to my room. Happily my
linen was neatly arranged in my black box,
and I had only a few things to collect and
pack up in the other; for, as my excitement
subsided, my heart was torn with mortification, and scalding tears so blinded me that
I could scarcely see what I was doing.
Mrs. Gower was not in sight when I went
downstairs; but the servant met me and
put an envelope in my hand. It contained
a cheque, with a few words to say that I
should find that the equivalent of the
quarter's salary due the '15th proximo,'
and requesting me to send a receipt at my
'earliest convenience.' I put the cheque
and note back in the envelope, and, being
not yet mistress of myself, I tore the envelope and enclosure in two pieces, and bade
the girl give it back to Mrs. Gower.

' Yes, miss,' she replied, taking the pieces. ' And mistress says shall she send your luggage to your address, or will you send for it ?'

I told her I would send for it ; and accordingly at the station I engaged a porter to fetch my two boxes ; and, after waiting in the dismal waiting-room in the darkest corner I could find for an hour and twenty minutes, I took my seat in the train and made the journey to London.

I have been in this hotel sixteen hours— the most wretched of my life. It seemed to me that I could not be more unhappy than when he was driving me to Marlow. Yet how happy was I then by comparison ! There I was beside him, here I am only with the memory of his presence. The appointments of the room remind me of the evening when we were here together—when I first discovered that I loved him ; and those

recollections of that happiness make the
misery of my present solitude greater.
Now, indeed, I have not one friend ; and it
is almost a crime to think of the man I
love.

Alas, I find that writing of my misfortunes, instead of exhausting the subject, as
I hoped, does but raise up new reflections
upon my miserable lot ! I have no courage.
I am beaten down and cowed. I cannot
even try to forget, now. I have tried and
tried to do so until, with repeated failure,
my head grows dizzy, and a kind of mad
despair seizes me. How can I forget ?
What thought can take a stronger hold
upon my mind than these that haunt me ?
In the street below there is perpetual movement—hundreds of people, men and women,
old and young, coming and going inces-
santly. Some appear absolutely without
thought, some bustle along, full of energy

and vigour, some stroll idly, some stop to
chat and laugh—it seems as though I alone,
amidst them all, am forlorn and weighed
down with despondency and grief.

 * * * * *

I am ashamed to have written the above.
Whilst I was walking up and down the
room, sobbing and wringing my hands like
a weak little fool, and saying to myself that
I had not a friend in the world, some one
knocked at my door ; and I had barely time
to slip my sodden handkerchief out of sight
when Mr. Gower entered the room.

'Why, my dear little girl, what's all this
about—eh?' he asked, setting his shiny hat
on the table and coming towards me briskly.
'Come—I'm old enough to be your father,
and, begad, you're nice enough to be my
own daughter ; so give me a kiss and tell
me all about it! There, there—don't cry,
unless you feel it will do you a lot of good,

for it's spoiling your pretty eyes and up-
setting me into the bargain. Sit you down
there, dear, with your back to the glaring
sun, and I'll pull up my chair beside you,
and we'll see what can be done to lighten
your heart and mine too. Do you mind
my having a little sherry and a biscuit
here? Thanks. I'll take the liberty to
ring the bell at once. Haven't had anything since twelve o'clock; and I'm getting
doocid peckish!' Saying this, he rang the
bell, and, pulling off his black kid gloves,
seated himself beside me. 'I should never
have thought of hunting for you here; but
I saw Linton this morning, and he put me
on the scent, you know.'

Hearing that, my heart began to beat
violently. It was evident he knew all, and
that Gilbert had sent him to me. I started
in my chair, eager to hear more. Mr.
Gower took no notice, or pretended not to

notice, but slipped his gloves in the tail pocket of his frock-coat; and then, bending forward, with his hand still in his pocket, he proceeded :

' Halloa—what's this? Oh, ah—something from the gals for you, my dear !' and with that he drew out and placed in my hand three letters, and then went to the door to tell the servant to bring sherry and biscuits.

The letters were bulky—there were two sheets of paper in each, and the writing was crossed. One was from Edith, another from Beatrice, and the third from Maud, and all began ' Dear darling ducky.' Oh, how cruel of me to forget them and think I had no friends ! My heart ached with remorse or joy—I know not which. I wished to kiss the letters and clasp them to my heart, but, Mr. Gower returning, I could not for shame. But he saw the

change in my emotions. Patting my
shoulder as he sat down, he said :

'Come, that's better, little one! I shall
enjoy my sherry if you keep that look on
your face. You don't want to read those
letters at once, do you? If you do, I'd better
call again in two or three days, for hang
me if I think you'll get through 'em in
less! What on earth young girls can find
to say to each other when they've been
parted only a few hours, I can't tell! I
suppose, like canaries, you sing the same
song over and over again, or what seems
to be the same song to an observer who has
very little of the singing-bird in his own
composition. Oh, here's the sherry—pretty
quick! I believe these waiters know by
the look of me what I am in the habit of
taking, and get out the sherry glasses the
moment they see me, for they never keep
me waiting. That'll do, Thomas. I'll

pour it. Never mind about the change. Shut the door after you. Thanks.—I think we shall find this a little more fortifying than Mrs. G.'s, my dear,' he said, handing a glass of wine to me. 'Let's chink glasses —so. Now try one of these little biscuits, and we'll get to business.'

He nodded kindly as I took a little sip of wine, and, crossing one fat little leg over the other, rubbed his hands, which were also fat, smiling approval when I broke the biscuit he had given me. I tried to eat; but it seemed as if I could never swallow the morsel I had taken; and, as I thought of his kindness in coming to see me, and of the affection of his dear daughters, whom I had lately thought never to hear of again, my spirits gave way, and I suddenly burst into tears, and once more I had to bring out my drabbled handkerchief.

'Tut, tut, tut! Why, what is there to

cry about, you poor little soul?' said Mr.
Gower, drawing his chair nearer to mine
and taking my hand in his. 'Sure-ly you
don't take to heart what that ill-bred, ill-
tempered, vindictive old catamaran said to
you, do you!' I shook my head. 'I
should think not,' he pursued. 'We've a
little too much sense for that. If words
could do it, she would have made me the
most miserable man under the sun; but
I am not exactly that, am I? Lord, what
is all her windy explosion like but the
popping of a paper bag, that may startle
children at first hearing, but amuses 'em
afterwards! We can afford to laugh at
her, eh—we who know her and value her
for what she is worth?' It made me smile
through my tears to hear his valiant
language now, and contrast it with his
timorous behaviour in her presence. 'I
promise you, my dear, I gave her such a

rating when I found you were gone last
night, as she is not likely to forget in a
hurry.' That made me smile again ; it was
so unlikely. ' As for the other affair, my
dear, can't you comfort yourself with the
reflection that it is not half so bad as it
might have been, and that there are
hundreds and thousands of women in this
city who have greater misfortunes than
yours to bear, and with no hope of ever
seeing the end of 'em on this side the grave
—though that's a source of comfort which
you, I believe, are not selfish enough to
enjoy thoroughly! You have the satisfaction of knowing that you have come out
blameless from the severest trial that a
young and single girl could be put to.
That's something, you know. Then you're
wonderful pretty, and you're quite young ;
you stand to win a good husband, and be
the happiest of women before a year's out.

Oh, but I know better!' he protested when I shook my head. 'Those gals of mine adore you; and do you think the young fellows will be behind them in discovering your admirable qualities? I'd lay any odds that in two months from now you'll have a round dozen of 'em at your heels, and any one of 'em a better man than Linton!'

'Oh, no, no, no!' I cried.

'Well, my dear, our opinions differ; and I think my age and experience justifies me in thinking yours wrong. He had the grace to confess all to me last night; and I can't think him blameless by his own showing, or believe that he's the sort of man to make such a delicate girl as you happy. I don't say that he's altogether bad, or even as bad as his version of this business would lead me to suppose; and I don't say that, if he had married you instead of Elgitha, either of you would ever have had cause to repent, for he was as fine a fellow as ever breathed before he got mixed up with these cursed Gauntlys. They'd ruin anyone not blessed with such 'an iron and brass-bound leather constitution as mine; and a proof of that Linton has given you in the most palpable form. A married man has no right to fall in love, no matter how wicked his wife may be, or however sweet and pretty the young lady with whom he is brought in contact. It's reprehensible—it's wrong!' Mr. Gower drew me to him, and, having kissed my forehead, said, with stern emphasis, ' It's very wrong indeed !'

' He could not help it any more than I can,' I said.

' Well, I suppose he couldn't, poor devil!' said Mr. Gower, smoothing my hand tenderly. ' Good heavens !' he

exclaimed, with a sigh. 'You, my dear,
may well count yourself the least unhappy
when you compare your lot with his! A
young fellow, in the full flush of manhood
and vigour, of a sympathetic and com-
panionable nature, not without a certain
amount of pride and ambition, linked for
life to a woman with the falsehood, cunning,
and vices of a very Jezebel, forced to give
up friends and position to avoid public
scandal, and compelled to crush out from
his heart every drop of warm blood that
might animate it with love and hope—he
is indeed to be pitied! It's hard enough
for a man of my age, with three dear
gals and—and a few other sources of
comfort, to have a wretch of a wife; but
for one not old enough to appreciate the
solace of good living, and not caring very
much for loo, what is there to render
existence tolerable? Nothing! And, to

put an end to such an intolerable existence,
nine men out of ten would, in one way
or another, kill themselves—the tenth would
kill his wife.'

'What will he do?' I asked, trembling.

'Oh, Linton? He's altogether an excep-
tional man! He'll let his wife kill him!
But what has that to do with it? I don't
want to excite your sympathy with him—
I have been carried away by fellow-feeling
into expressing ideas and sentiments which
you must not allow yourself to share.
You must confine yourself to self-con-
gratulations on being better off than he
is, if you can. That's what I started with
the intention of impressing upon you.
There—put away that handkerchief, and
let us talk reasonably and practically!
You feel better now, don't you?'

'Yes. I am not going to be stupid any
more.'

'That's right. Well, now, I have come here as a man of business, as a bank-manager, to make some sort of reparation for the conduct of my wife. She gave me one account—which of course I don't believe a word of—and the girls have given me another, which they had from Betsy, who happened to have her ear at the key-hole during your interview with Mrs. G.— and that I can believe. Of course the gals know all about this ; for, in the first place, we were all in the boat together when Linton hailed me from the bank, and walked me off to lay the whole matter before me; and, in the second place, they got hold of my razor and my strop and wouldn't let me shave myself this morning until I had let 'em into the secret. I thought, you know, my dear,' he said nervously, 'as you are so open with them, and there's no likelihood of their telling their ma, you would not mind my giving way.'

'No. I am glad they know.'

'Well, we were all pleased with your behaviour. "It's just like ducky," said Trix. "I know she'd die rather than do what she thought was wrong." Then Edith fired up ; and, says she, "Yes, and ducky'd die rather than say a word that should make anyone think ill of Gilbert!" And we were all glad that you tore the cheque in half and sent it back to the old woman. You may be sure she didn't mention a word of that to me, but led me to suppose that you had received your salary in full ; and we're glad for one reason, and one reason only, that you would not stay in the house after the impertinent conduct of Mrs. G. So far, so good. But you must understand, my dear, that I am master of my house, and

am responsible for the conduct of my
family. If anyone employed in my house
is ill-used, it is my duty to make compensa-
tion. I don't wish to offend your delicacy.
I am not going to put so many pounds,
shillings, and pence in your hand. What
I intend doing is to find you a home for
the one you have lost, and to see that you
do not suffer by having given your services
to my family. I might lose my position
as a bank-manager if I did less. Oh,
indeed I might—it's perfectly true! The
money due to you I shall put to your
credit at the bank ; and, when you have
need of a few pounds, you will only have
to ask for it there, and it will be given
you. Here's a little book of forms that
you will fill up as you think fit.' He
laid a long narrow book on the table as
he spoke ; and then, turning again to me,
he continued, seeing my embarrassment and

surprise, 'We won't talk about that any more. You are too sensible a girl to be swayed by false notions of delicacy. What I have done is purely a matter of necessity as a man of business. Now let me talk to you in the pleasanter aspect of a friend. You have no very great desire to stay in this hotel, I suppose?'

'Oh no! I came here because——'

'Because it was respectable, and you'd been here before; just so. That's how I came to find you. Thought you would. Of course, you haven't had time to think of any future occupation.'

'I—I have had time, but—but——'

'Not much inclination. You can't decide on such a subject quickly. Best to take plenty of time for consideration. We can look about us as soon as you get a little stronger. The first thing is to get you into a comfortable home, where you can

talk out all that's in your heart to some
one who can sympathize with you and
understand your position; isn't it?'

I nodded. A warm glow seemed to
spread over me as I listened to this
suggestion.

'Well, in that case, as soon as you are
yourself again—to-morrow, say—we will
go together and see my mother-in-law.
Don't be startled; it's no relation of the
present Mrs. G.'s. It's my first wife's
mother. I dare say the girls have told
you about granny.' I nodded again, with
rising hope, for how often have the girls
talked to me about her in my bedroom!
'She's a dear old soul, and just as fond
of young folk as they are of her. She is no
more fitted for solitude than you are; and
for some time we've been on the look-out
for some pleasant person who could lodge
with her. It seems to me that you and she

are exactly fitted for each other. She's a gentlewoman by nature, just as you are, my dear; and, if she hasn't the fine habits of the present Mrs. G., she certainly has not her coarse feelings. Granny keeps a shop, you know. That's enough to keep Mrs. G. at a distance; so you may meet the gals there as often as they can get that way without fear of being annoyed by their ma. There's a little bit of a garden behind the house, and the rooms are as neat and nice as hands can make 'em.'

'I know. I have heard all about that!' I cried joyfully, clasping my hands.

'There are two spare rooms set aside for my gals, which granny would be very glad to let you have, for while they are empty they remind her of the breach my folly in marrying Mrs. Gauntly has made in the family; and I think we can persuade her to take a reasonable price for them.

Of course you'll have to pay her, you know.'

' Oh, of course !'

' And you like the idea ?'

' Oh, yes !'

' Very well ; then now all you have to do is to get yourself presentable, so that granny shall like the look of you, and be brought to rational terms for her rooms. Do you think you shall look all right to-morrow ?'

' I will.   I won't cry any more.'

' That's right.   I shall come for you at three, so that we may be in time to take tea with granny.   And, if you only agree to live together, I'll promise both of you that the gals shall spend a couple of days at Kennington the first week they come back to London, whether Mrs. G. likes it or not.'

CHAPTER IV.

THE DIARY.—THE SCENE CHANGES.

EPTEMBER 24 (Kennington).—
I fear I have the qualities of a very
selfish friend. When solitude
has oppressed my spirits, when my joy was
not to be contained in silence, when I have
been wretched and yearned to pour out my
grief in words, I have turned to these pages ;
but now, having no such need for relief, I
neglect my poor old book. I have been here
a week, and to-night, for the first time, I
have bethought myself of it.

My face was wretchedly pale, and my

eyes were still a little red, when Mr. Gower
came to fetch me, though I had not shed
one tear from the time of his leaving me the
day before. I was so anxious that granny
—I can think of Mrs. Simpson only by that
name—should not take a dislike to me from
my ill-looks, that I believe I could have
repressed my tears had I felt disposed to
cry. But indeed I had no such disposition,
for, having made up my mind to think only
of the hopeful possibilities of my future life
and kept my resolution, I grew more composed and reasonable as the day advanced,
slept well at night, and woke without that
terrible numbness in my heart which I had
felt since the first great shock of my grief.

'Do you think Mrs. Simpson will like
me?' I asked Mr. Gower, as he held my
hands in his and looked at me approvingly.

'I'll disown her if she doesn't,' he replied.
'I don't know anyone who wouldn't like

you, my dear—except my wife ; and, thank
Heaven, there's not such another as she in
this world !'

I was glad to hear that, but still I felt a
little anxious ; and, when Mr. Gower held
up his umbrella and waved it towards the
pavement as a signal to the cabman to stop,
I looked out of the little side-window with
eager curiosity to see what kind of house
granny lived in. We were close to it—an
old red-brick house, with green boxes of
flowers at the upper windows, and an old-
fashioned bow-fronted shop, with small
panes of glass very bright and clean, the
name of 'Simpson' along the top, with
'Biscuit' going up one side and 'Baker'
going down the other. In the window were
about ten little baskets full of biscuits. A
cat, with her paws tucked under her breast,
was asleep by the side of the door. The
level of the street was higher than the floor,

so one had to descend a step to enter the
shop. I noticed a sweet wholesome smell
of fresh-baked biscuits as I crossed the
threshold, and the next moment I stood face
to face with granny. There was no need of
an introduction ; no one but she could be
the mistress of such a house, or the person
whose character I had learnt from the loving
praises of her granddaughters. A spare tall
old lady, just a little bent with age, with a
very fair skin, delicate features, and a bright
cheerful expression upon her face—such was
Mrs. Simpson. She wore sleeves and apron,
and a plain white cap. from which projected
on either side of her face two short silvery
curls. She must have been apprised of my
coming, for, after regarding me for a moment,
she said :

'Your name is Gertrude, my dear?'

'Yes,' I replied.

'I am very glad to see you,' she said,

and, giving me her hand, she led me into the little parlour at the back of the shop—a rather dark little room, but with a window opening upon a small garden gay with bright-coloured flowers, and an open view of the shop and the street, which renders it extremely cheerful and interesting. It was a great relief to my eyes to get out of the glaring light, and it was a satisfaction to know that the traces of my recent suffering would be less obvious to granny. I hardly remember what we talked about at first; I only know that the more I heard of her sweet voice, and the more I saw of the little parlour, with its corner cupboards of china, its bevelled glass, its excessive neatness, and the air of repose that pervaded it, the more I hoped that I might stay with her and make my home there. Granny rang the bell, and a particularly prim little maid, with a face that shone like a well-polished

apple, and a white apron and print dress so
excessively starched that they stuck out as
if they were made of tin, came to the door.
This queer child, being instructed to lead
me to the spare room, responded by the
queerest little curtsey imaginable, her legs
seeming to give way at the knees for an
instant, and recovering their rigidity as
suddenly as they had lost it. She took me
upstairs, and there, with another little bob,
left me.

This spare room is now my bed-chamber.
The window looks out upon the road. The
muslin curtains are drawn back with blue
ribbons ; the dressing-table has a kind of
valance of blue glazed material covered with
muslin ; the dimity curtains and the hang-
ings to the bed are white, with a little blue
spray of forget-me-nots. No room in the
world could be more bright and cheerful.
I fancy the dear old lady must have con-

sulted her grandchildren's taste in furnishing
it, with the hope that they would occupy it
frequently, for, except in the prim arrangement, there is nothing antiquated or out of
character with the present time. As soon
as I had smoothed my hair I went downstairs, and found the tea-things laid and an
urn hissing and steaming upon the table.
Granny was in the shop, serving a very
stout old gentleman with a bag of biscuits,
and he was telling her how many years he
had dealt with her, and complaining of the
changes that had taken place in the neigh-
bourhood. Nearly all granny's customers
are alike—very sober, respectable, and pleasant old gentlemen and ladies, who like to
linger over their purchases, recalling past
times and comparing their memories with
hers, deploring the degeneracy of Kennington, and the difficulty of buying things now
as good as they used to be. I have seen

only one new customer, and she seemed to
think it was very odd that granny should
sell nothing but biscuits, advised · her to
have the shop altered, and to add fancy
bread and pastry to her stock, and promised
to recommend her to several friends if
she found her bread, etc., equal to the
biscuits she had tasted. But granny does
not want new customers. ' The old ones
will last as long as I,' she says ; she does
not care to be patronized, and she does not
want to alter her old shop or her old ways,
and, I think, has an opinion that she can
manage her business as well as any younger
person could manage it for her.

When the tea-things were removed, Mr.
Gower went into the little garden to smoke
a cigar; then granny drew her chair close
to mine, and, smiling kindly, said:

' Do you think you should like to stay in
Kennington a little while, my dear?'

'I think I should like to live here always,' I replied; 'it is so quiet and restful.'

She looked at me thoughtfully, with a shade of sadness in her eyes. I was thinking that this old-fashioned, still place was just such as old maids might choose to live in, and I think she saw what was in my thoughts.

'Young people find it dull here after a little time, and then they want to be gone.'

'I shall not want to go away. It must be very beautiful to live a quiet, even life, to go from day to day through a routine of duties that one's strength is equal to, and find contentment in that. If one is content, that is everything.'

'Ah, my love, who is content? It is not enough merely to live; even an old woman sighs for something more than that.

We must suffer, we must endure, we must
hope until the last ; only, as our strength
fails, we suffer and hope less. Do you see
the empty cage that hangs by the garden-
wall there ? In the winter my cat caught
a poor sparrow that had grown weak and
tame through hunger and cold, and, rather
proud of his performance, Tom brought the
maimed little creature to me. Its wing was
hurt, but it still lived ; so I sent out for
that cage and kept it a prisoner until its wing
was strong and the sun shone warm. Then
I opened the door and it flew away, and
never returned to me. Day by day you
will grow stronger, my love ; and one
bright day you will seek a brighter home
than this.'

Ah, granny cannot know how deeply I
have loved!

'However,' she continued, in a gayer
tone, after a little sigh, 'as you like the

place, the question now to be considered is whether you will like me.'

' Oh, I am quite sure of that!'

' Old women are tedious and crotchety, and believe that their judgment in certain matters is superior to that of young folk. which often makes them exacting and difficult to please.'

' I don't think I shall find it difficult to please you. I know it will be a pleasure to try.'

' That is a very pretty remark, my dear. prompted, I am sure, by a very sweet feeling. If we begin by trying to please each other, we shall end by pleasing each other without trying. Would you like to begin soon?'

' Yes, as soon as possible. You cannot think how wretched it is to be alone in a great hotel full of people who never speak to you.'

'There is no reason why you should return to the hotel. There is a drawer full of linen that I keep well aired in case my grandchildren should come unexpectedly. You can use that until your own is sent on from the hotel.'

I caught granny's soft-skinned thin hand and pressed it, my heart full to overflowing with gratitude. But we had said nothing as to the price I was to pay, and this I hinted at as well as I could.

'I intend that you shall pay, my dear,' she replied, 'for, though it will be a great comfort to me to have a companion, I do not wish you to be under any feeling of obligation to me. On the contrary, I should like the advantage to be on my side, so that you may be under no constraint in speaking if you feel that your position here is irksome, and that you would like one with more life and change. How much you must pay I cannot tell you now. As you may suppose, I am scrupulous about money-matters, and keep my accounts very exactly; so that at the end of a month I shall be able to tell to a nicety how much you have cost me, and that will serve as a guide for your future payments.'

'Well, have you finished the bargain yet?' asked Mr. Gower, coming to the window and leaning upon the sill, with a very large cigar in the corner of his mouth and a straw hat tilted over one eye. Granny keeps this hat for his use.

'Yes, yes,' I cried; 'it is all settled! I'm not going back to the hotel.'

'You're a nice grateful young party, upon my soul! You seem quite pleased to think I must go back to town alone. Partly your doings, madam.' He turned his twinkling little eye upon granny, and turned his cigar from one corner of his mouth to the other. 'Never mind; I'll be revenged. I'll go to the very wickedest theatre that's open.'

'And the sooner the better, if we are to be poisoned with smoke while you stay here,' retorted granny, with spirit.

'You won't escape then. I've given a couple of the strongest cigars I had to that old rascal William'—William is the baker, who has been in granny's service thirty-five years. 'Well, my dear,' he said, taking the cigar out of his mouth and throwing it away, 'I'm glad you're going to stay here, for your own sake, and for yours equally, Mrs. Simpson.'

Granny made him a little mock curtsey, and so that matter ended. Soon afterwards Mr. Gower went away, after giving a shilling to Jane, the apple-faced maid, and half-a-crown to that 'old rascal' William, who

had fetched a cab, and could not look at
him without a chuckle and a little sidelong
jerk of his head, which seemed to say, ' Oh,
you are a witty gentleman!' I wonder what
Mrs. Gower would think of her husband's
behaviour, she who never, to my knowledge,
gave a farthing to anyone, and maintained
that servants should only be treated with
severity and 'kept in their place.'

No existence could be more calm and
tranquil than mine now. Everything is
orderly and regular; and yet one is never
made uncomfortable by a sense of restric-
tion and suppression such as Mrs. Gower's
stringent regulations caused. Were I naturally untidy and careless—I don't think I
am very—I should be neat and orderly
instinctively in granny's house, and with
her example before me. At seven o'clock
we rise, and at eight we sit down to breakfast—tea, a pat of fresh butter, a little

brown loaf, two eggs or rashers of toasted
bacon, served on a cloth as smooth, white,
and spotless as possible. The most pressing
affairs of the day are done between breakfast
and dinner. After that granny dozes for
half-an-hour, and then sets herself to read
one of her favourite books—'Pickwick,'
which she enjoys heartily; 'The Voyages of
Captain Cook,' in three ponderous volumes;
and the 'Pilgrim's Progress,' which sometimes tickles her sense of humour, though
I cannot see how or why, and sometimes
excites a feeling of veneration and devo-
tion.

But she loves most to chat; and if I have
not a book in my hand she will glance over
the top of her glasses now and then at me,
and with increasing frequency, until at last
she closes her book, and, drawing off her
spectacles with a queer little twitch of her
eyelids, says:

'Now, lovey, let us have a little gossip about things in general.'

After tea, William, in his white cap and apron, comes into the shop, and granny and I go out for a walk. And a very pleasant part of the day's routine this is, for granny has something pleasant to say—some sage reflection, or sweet or humorous remark about anything that we chance to regard, no matter how insignificant in itself the thing is. She is very widely known, and no royal person 'walking abroad'—that is one of her phrases—could receive more frequent marks of respect, nor acknowledge them with more becoming grace.

At half-past eight we have supper—bread and butter, with cream-cheese or some fruit; and after that Jane comes into the parlour and takes her seat in the corner, and granny reads a chapter of the Bible aloud. William has been present at this ceremony once; but on other evenings he has gone out for a stroll, and to smoke his pipe, which he prefers.

'The comfort of piety is less necessary to men than to us women,' granny tells me, in explanation of his defection. And then we separate, granny and I, with a kiss and kindly wishes, and go to bed.

Surely, under such favourable conditions, I ought to be happy—or, if not happy, at least not discontented with my lot! And yet, when I lie down at night, my heart is heavy; and it is not light when I rise in the morning. There must be some foolish or evil bent in my disposition. Why else, when my reason tells me I should rejoice, does my heart repine? It is madness to grieve because that is not which never could have been. It is wicked to think of him, yet my heart glows, as I write, with un-

quenched love. I have prayed and prayed
for strength to think of him no more, until
my rebellious thoughts have made the prayer
a mockery.

CHAPTER V.

NOVEMBER 11 (Kennington).— There has been a very thick fog to-day, the first I have ever seen. Granny would have kept me at home, but I would not be persuaded by the dear soul. It was with difficulty I assured myself that I had not lost my way; and, had it not been for the brass plate on the gate, I could not have distinguished the school, where I now have an employment as teacher of French, from the houses on either side. Nearly all the day-scholars were absent. Miss Fletcher scolded me for coming, whilst praising me for my attendance ; and, as soon as it grew a little less dense, insisted upon my going home.

I was surprised to hear that Mr. Gower had visited granny this morning. 'A little matter of business brought him, my dear,' she said; but that made his coming only the more odd, since business in the ordinary way is about the last thing in the world that would make him undertake such an unpleasant journey. Granny has been grave all day. I hope, with all my heart, that this business matter is not the cause. It would not surprise me to find that she is pinched for money, for trade is worse now than ever—ladies and gentlemen being afraid to go out in such weather as we have had since October—and she cannot sell enough biscuits in a week to pay William's wages.

November 15.—Thank Heaven, the fears
I had lately on granny's account were
ill-founded! This being half-holiday—
Wednesday — I left Miss Fletcher's at
twelve o'clock, and, thinking of nothing in
particular — except it was that the fallen
chestnut-leaves smelt very nice, that it was
pleasant to see a little sunlight once more
after the horrid fogs, that it is very droll
to keep ringing a bell when one has muffins
to sell, or on some such unimportant subject—and had just passed the corner of
Audrey Road, when I was nearly scared
out of my senses by the three girls,
Beatrice, Edith, and Maud, bouncing down
upon me like great tomboys as they are,
from the wall by the doctor's, where they
had been waiting in ambush for me. I
think I am getting cross as well as old.
Certainly it takes less to irritate me now
than it used to. I felt quite angry with the

girls for frightening me, instead of being delighted to see them.

'You shouldn't do that!' I said, kissing them all the same. 'There are two ladies on the other side of the way who look quite astounded.'

'Oh, isn't ducky proper now she's a governess?' exclaimed Beatrice.

'Hush, Miss Gow-ah!' said Edith, with mock severity. 'Don't you know that walls have e-ars, and that "ducky" is not your teach-ah's proper name?'

'I vote we walk two and two, and be careful to keep our eyes before us,' said Maud.

'Don't be stupid!—I didn't mean to be cross—but you frightened me,' I said, with another kiss at each break, where I have put a dash, for one of them. 'Why, who could have expected to see you? Where's Gwenny?'

'Oh, she's gone with ma! That's why we're here.'

'The enemy's retired in complete disorder,' said Maud, with a triumphant flourish of her hand.

'And the first thing we did when Gwenny told us they weren't coming back to-day, was to look in Bradshaw and find out how we were to get from Camden Road to Clapham with the least delay.'

'Yes, and we made up our mind to startle you as you were going home.'

'And we did.'

'We are a happy family!' said Edith; and then the two cried out in chorus, 'We are, we are, we are!'—and the two ladies on the other side of the way must have been more shocked than before. For my part, I could not help laughing at the exuberant spirits of these dear girls. Edith and Trix had hold of my arms; Maud,

compelled to take an outside place,
said :

'Very good, my dear children. I warn
you that, if I'm to go outside to oblige you
now, I shall sleep with ducky to-night.'

'Are you going to stay all night ?' I
asked.

'Of course we are ! We're going to take
granny by storm. Won't she open her
eyes and lift up her dear old hands in
surprise to see us marching in ?'

'Oh, I'll tell you what! Ducky shall
go in first; then, when we've counted fifty,
Trix shall go in; then Edith shall follow
after another fifty ; and, when I've counted
the same, I'll walk in. Granny'll think
there's never going to be an end to the
gang !'

'Gang !' said I.

'Is that very wrong, ducky? So sorry !
I meant " crew." '

Thus they rattled on, one piece of nonsense after another, until at length they all ceased, as if from exhaustion. Then I asked where Mrs. Gower was gone.

'To Marlow.'

'Marlow!' I exclaimed, with a strange trembling, and wondering what could possibly take Mrs. Gower there at this time of the year.

'Haven't you heard?'

'Don't you know what's happened?'

'Didn't pa tell you when he came last week?'

'No,' I replied, more and more astonished by these rapid questions. 'What has happened?'

'Why, Elgitha has run away from the Abbey!'

'Run away?'

'Yes, with Barton—Gilbert's servant—a

base, wicked woman! I knew she'd do
something shameful in the end.'

I remembered Barton, the handsome
servant that had waited upon us when we
were crossing the Channel, and I remembered his covert unpleasant glances at me
from behind his master's chair.

'Ma don't know that she's run away
with a footman, or, if she does, she pretends
not to know. Gilbert has said nothing
about it.'

'That's characteristic of him, poor old
fellow!' said Beatrice. 'He never has said
a word about his wife's faults. He just lets
people think that he's cruel and tyrannical
to his wife, and suffers ma to circulate
whatever rumours it may please her to
invent, without attempting to throw the
blame off himself upon Elgitha by showing
what a vile creature she is.'

'I wish some one would tell the whole

truth. Pa ought to ; but he *is such* a coward!'

' He told us. The lawyer engaged by ma to investigate matters found it out and told him, you know, ducky. Gilbert has not said a word even to the lawyer engaged against him.'

' Against him ?' I said, in astonishment.

' Yes. It's an awful blow to ma to have it supposed even that Elgitha has run away from her husband. People would imagine that she did not run away alone, and there'd be an end of ma's status in the snobocracy. People couldn't be proud of knowing the ma of Lady Linton if it was widely conjectured that Lady Linton had brought shame upon her husband. Ma'd be at a discount.'

' Take a back row at once.'

' It would be as bad for her as if pa were to open a butcher's shop.'

' What a bit of fun *that* would be !'

' Hush, Edith !' said I.

' Well, one may as well say a thing as feel it ; and I know we should all rejoice in our hearts at ma's mortification. I don't see anything to respect, let alone revere, in a woman who's just as snobbish in her own circle as the Jews at Margate. Fine airs and coarse feelings are the very essence of vulgarity. What do you think, ducky ? Don't you think that we three girls, though we do use slang, and are rough and rude, are less vulgar than ma ?'

' But what can Mrs. Gower do to injure Sir Gilbert Linton ?' I asked. 'If Lady Linton has gone away, and her husband refuses to ascribe a reason, it seems to me that nothing more can be said.'

' That shows how little you know of ma. She'd do the wickedest, meanest thing in

the world to save herself from falling in the
estimation of her friends and admirers.
Look what a triumph it would be to all the
little sycophants who court her society now,
if they could cut her dead in " society " or
snub her anyhow ! They hate each other
like cats in a bag, these superfine superi-ah
Camden Sq-are ladies !'

' You haven't answered ducky's question
as to what ma's doing to injure Gilbert.
She's trying to make it suspected that
Gilbert has murdered Elgitha.'

' Oh !'

' Isn't it shameful ? You see, ducky,
when our sweet step-sister bolted with her
husband's footman and her jewels, she
thought it best to get the river between
herself and Sir Gilbert as soon as possible.
So the boat was taken from the boathouse,
and, when it had carried her across, it was
left to float down with the current. The

wreck of it was found the next morning at the foot of a weir.'

' Is it known that she crossed ?' I asked, with a faltering voice.

'Oh yes ! She and the footman were seen twice afterwards. Of course no one is supposed to know that. The solicitor told pa, because he thought pa was as greatly interested as ma in proving Sir Gilbert guilty of murder.'

' And because pa'll have to pay the solicitor's fees,' suggested Maud.

' Ma will move heaven and earth to save her daughter's reputation. You may be sure she will find means to suppress the rumours that Lady Linton has been seen since the night she left the Abbey. The solicitor hinted to pa that a certain sum of money judiciously spent would make those people who saw Elgitha doubt their own senses, and believe that they were mistaken. Ma's put us all in deep mourning.

'But we took it off as soon as she was out of the house this morning.'

'Yes; and she's gone down to Marlow to show her crape. People always believe in crape, you know; and I believe, if a hundred witnesses were to swear they had seen Elgitha, the world would point to ma's crape and say it was impossible.'

'I wish it was not mean to write anonymous letters. I should like to let everyone in ma's visiting-list know the whole truth.'

'It's an awful shame! Poor Gilbert! It seems as if there was never to be an end to his punishment for having trusted a woman.'

'Oh, I think he's less to be pitied now than before she left him! He's not obliged now to stop at the Abbey for fear she shall disgrace him in his absence. He must have expected such an event. We know for certain that he has had to keep her a prisoner since that abominable affair at Brighton.'

'Ducky doesn't know anything about that.'

'It isn't the sort of thing ducky would care to hear. It's one of those scandals that we are supposed not to understand, you know, dear ; but Trix has a cutting from a Brighton paper, given her by Laura Drake, who was there at the time, and that puts it plain enough for a child to comprehend. Mr. Drake knows the proprietor of the paper, and he was told that Gilbert bought up the whole edition of the paper, and paid a heavy sum that no further reference should be made to his wife's shame.'

'Surely, with no evidence against Sir Gilbert, Mrs. Gower dare not openly accuse him of having killed his wife ?' I ventured

to say. 'It is an absurd, preposterous
charge!'

'Catch ma doing anything of that kind
openly! Don't you know her way, ducky—
how she will pretend to give no opinion,
and yet cunningly lead people to suppose
the very worst?'

They talked for some time, but I did not
catch all they said, my mind being
charged with more food than it could at
once digest.

'And he?' I asked after a while. 'What
has become of him?'

'He is at the Abbey. Pa has not seen
him, and he only wrote a formal note
acknowledging the receipt of pa's note and
our messages. I am not surprised; he
must hate the whole lot of us. I suppose
he will wait until the result of the investigation is known, and then I should think
he would go abroad to live. I would. I

should detest every person and thing that could remind me of such a woman. We shall never see him again.'

' Oh, poor Gilbert !'

My heart echoed that cry.

' And now do let us talk of something else,' said Beatrice.

November 20.—No news. I think granny must have scolded the girls for telling me so much. She knows that my heart is un-healed ; but how should they understand my feelings—they who fall in love twenty times in the year, and seem never better pleased than when they have a new flirtation to talk about ? I dare say they know what happened in September, and look upon it simply as a rather improper legerity on the part of their step-brother-in-law, which I have long ago forgotten. In answering my letter of the 18th, Beatrice alludes as briefly as possible to the questions I asked.

'I'm sorry, dear,' she writes, 'that I cannot answer all your questions. There is nothing to tell. Ma is at home posing as a very ugly and stony kind of Niobe. Pa says she has prudently called off the dogs of law, seeing that they were likely to serve her as Actæon's hounds served him. You will be glad to see that I do not neglect my " Mangnall's Questions,"' and so on.

Granny watches me closely, and is kinder, if possible, than ever, doing all that is in her power to divert my thoughts from sombre reflections and turn them into bright channels. She knows that my love is not extinguished, and that the old look about my face and my sober mien are not the mere result of teaching French. Poor granny! Solicitude for my welfare makes it difficult for her to be silent upon the subject which she perceives occupies my

mind, while instinctive good taste withholds
her from speaking. It is easy to see which
way her thoughts tend. She spoke in com-
passionate terms last night of those persons
whose follies or vices make them the detes-
tation of the world, and hinted significantly
at our duty towards them.

'Is there anyone in the world, my love,'
she said, 'so miserable as they—without
hope, without the pleasant recollection of a
single good action, without one loving
friend, without the slightest consolation in
their wretchedness? Would the most unhappy of those who suffer from the faults of
others change places for a moment with them,
who suffer only by their own wickedness?
How are we to judge them? How are we
to say what share of blame is theirs? Not
by our own standard, for, maybe, we have had
neither their temptations nor their feebleness
to withstand. We must make allowances

for them, as we should for children who do
wrong, or persons of unsound mind. I
cannot help believing that the tendency to
evil is something beyond our own control,
and that the love of evil-doing is a kind of
mania; and those so afflicted are surely to
be pitied and helped. Don't you think so,
love? And we must admire those persons
who, having the misfortune to be connected
with such people, renounce selfish desires and
inclinations in order to rescue them from the
misery of their own creating, and prevent
them, if possible, from falling lower, just as
we must blame and hold in contempt others
who abandon them to their fate in order to
pursue their own personal pleasures.'

Granny misjudges him, thinking him
perhaps all to blame for my unhappiness,
and she forms an unjust estimate of his
character if she thinks he will neglect a duty
that is apparent to her. I have so much

confidence in him, that I write this without
fear that his act will make me blot it out in
shame. He will not seek me, now that he
might better justify himself in making me
an offer. It is granny only who starts
with anxiety when a step is heard upon the
threshold.

CHAPTER VI.

ARCH 25 (Kennington).—At last the long winter is ended. The window-boxes are bright with spring bulbs, snowdrops, and crocuses—the hyacinths are just showing colour—and the little parlour is fragrant with cut wall-flower. The sun has shone with great brilliancy, making the air quite warm in the middle of the day; and the atmosphere is so clear and bright that my thoughts have dwelt involuntarily upon the sea as I walked to school and back, and whenever my pupils suffered my attention to stray away from them. Granny seems a little unwell to-day; she complains that the east wind is not good for old bones, and is restless and nervous.

March 27.—Granny's anxiety continues. To-night, when I asked for the *Times*, which is usually brought after tea and left with us until the morning, she said, with some embarrassment, that it had not been delivered; but the moment after, unable to deceive me, or even to let me deceive myself, she added:

'My love, I will tell you why I have told the man not to bring the paper; it is because there is something in it which I do not wish you to read.'

She said no more; but it was enough to make me understand that there is bad news concerning *him*. Lady Linton has been discovered perhaps, and there is a repetition of the public scandal at which the girls hinted in the autumn. Granny must be right, and my curiosity to know what has happened is undoubtedly wrong. Nevertheless I cannot help hoping for a letter from the girls, or, better still, a visit.

March 29.— . . . . Letter from Maud, but no allusion to any uncommon occurrence. I found the *Times* upon the table this evening, and, as I might have assured myself, not a line in it concerning anyone of my acquaintance. After all, it may have been only an unpleasant case which granny, with characteristic nicety, considered improper reading for a young woman.

April 3.— . . . . Letter from Beatrice, most affectionate and sweet, but the most serious and least careless I have ever had from her. I believe it was composed and then copied—a thing quite unprecedented in the history of her correspondence with me. I feel sure that something has happened, or is now taking place, which I am not to know, which in some way affects me. Not only does Trix write in guarded terms, and granny find it impossible to fix her attention patiently on any one thing, but even Miss Fletcher regards me with a kind of considerate interest. She and granny do chat a great deal on half-holidays, and it is just possible that my affairs are not a secret from the best and most trustworthy of Mrs. Simpson's old friends. She may have thought it necessary to tell her all last autumn, when it was proposed that I should teach at Miss Fletcher's school. That just serves to increase my belief that some fact concerning *him* is being kept from my knowledge.

April 10.—This afternoon, as granny and I were sitting at tea, a cab drew up sharply before the door, and, before it had quite stopped, Mr. Gower, with a newspaper in his hand, jumped out and came hurrying to us.

'It's all right,' he began, as he crossed the shop, seeing our astonishment, or at least my astonishment—'it's all right— he's acquitted!'

'Acquitted!' I exclaimed. 'Of what?'

'Why, of murder, my dear! And thank Heaven for it!' he replied, pushing back his hat and wiping the perspiration from his forehead. 'There's the evening paper, granny; you'll find a line about it. Just come from Reading. Thought you'd be anxious to know how it had ended, so took a cab and came on straight. Give me a cup o' tea, there's a good soul! I'm pretty well exhausted with the excitement of the day, and that dam Underground Railway!'

'There is no occasion to use unpleasant

words, Joseph,' said granny gently, as she
opened the tea-caddy to prepare some fresh
tea for Mr. Gower.

' Beg pardon, granny! One may be
pardoned for giving vent to his feelings
after bottling 'em up so long !'

Granny shook her head gravely and
glanced at me anxiously, as if she thought
it would have been better for me had he
kept his feelings bottled up still longer, and
left me in ignorance. I had sunk into a
chair, and sat trembling with anxiety and I
know not what emotions—wishing to know
more, yet unable to ask a question. Mr.
Gower, following the direction of granny's
glance, caught sight of me; and, seeing my
condition, he started from his seat, came to
my side, and with great concern exclaimed,
as he took my hand :

' Why, my dear, what's the matter ?
Hang it all, I might have known ! And

yet the girls told me that you knew
all !'

'The girls are just as thoughtless as
you,' said granny. 'Gertrude knows
nothing of the dreadful business. Now
she must know all; and you had better
tell her while I make the tea.'

'Well, my dear,' said Mr. Gower, when
granny had left the room, 'with all due
respect to Mrs. Simpson, I see no harm in
your hearing all about it. While there was
a doubt as to the result of this trial, it was
right, of course, to keep you in the dark.
But good news can harm no one, I think;
and, to tell the truth, it was as much for
your sake as for granny's or my own that I
brought the news; for, though I concluded
from my own observation and the girls'
that you had ceased to have any—any feeling, you know, for Sir Gilbert, I felt sure
you would be glad to hear of his escape

from a very serious dilemma. The girls wouldn't have kept the secret long if I had. They couldn't. You must have found it out, or suspected something.'

'I have suspected something. There was something in the *Times* which granny did not wish me to see. I knew it referred to him.'

'Ah, that was an account of the inquest, perhaps! I'll begin at the beginning. You know that last November Lady Linton left the Abbey; that, after her departure, several honest people were prepared to swear that they had seen her with a man on the Oxford side of the river, or that they had not seen her, as their interest guided them? At the Monkden Weir the boat was found bottom up. It was concluded that, if Lady Linton were discovered, her body would take the same course as the boat; and accordingly all about the weir a great deal of search was made to no purpose. It must be admitted that the men who made this search did so with the foregone conclusion that they should find nothing—it being a matter of common notoriety amongst this lower class of people, who drew their information from the servants at the Abbey, that Lady Linton had eloped with her husband's valet — John Barton. Consequently their search was far less thorough and discriminating than if it had been made by unbiased and intelligent persons—the police, for example. My precious wife, as I have no doubt the girls told you, tried to establish the belief that her daughter had been murdered, and to a certain extent she succeeded. A great many friends supported her theory; and during the winter Mrs. Gower has been more popular than ever with that class of people she affects. Meanwhile Gilbert stayed at the Hall, perhaps to discountenance the rumours against him, perhaps to receive his wife if she repented and came back for forgiveness. He's Quixotic enough for anything when he's put on his metal. At any rate, he stayed there, which was certainly not the sort of thing a murderer would do.

'At the beginning of last month he gave orders that the boat-house, which had been flooded during the winter, should be put in repair. The workmen went there, threw open the gates and windows, and the master-man began to look about to see what was necessary. The first thing he noticed was a quantity of fur clinging to the scum and slime which had accumulated on the surface of the water and formed a kind of dam against the water-gates. His first idea was that a fox or some such creature had got under the gates at low water and been drowned there. But another workman noticed that there was not only fur, but long hair, in the slime. I see, my dear, that these details are unpleasant to you. They are revolting, and that's a fact; and, as they are not necessary, I'll say as little about 'em as possible. The long and short of it is that the place was dredged, and there they fished up the remains of Lady Linton.

'Gilbert identified the fur-lined cloak— of which a portion still remained intact— the watch, bracelets, etc., which were found amongst that awful mass of decomposition. Mrs. Gower was prepared to swear to each of the poor wretch's bones, of course. My dear, it's all right; I've come to an end of the horrible details. Beyond identifying the remains and giving the briefest possible account of his wife's disappearance, Gilbert gave no evidence at the inquest. The doctor who had attended Lady Linton declared that she had exhibited strong symptoms of insanity; and it was clear that Gilbert hoped that her death would be attributed to that cause. You can understand how repugnant to a man of his feelings it would be to expose his wife's vices, and make them the subject of public conversation.

'In all probability a verdict in accordance with the doctor's view of the case would have been returned, had it not been for my precious wife's interference. She protested that for a long time previous to her death Lady Linton had gone in fear of her life, and produced a quantity of letters from her daughter in which Gilbert was accused of violence, cruelty, and an intention to murder her; and upon that evidence the jury gave a verdict of wilful murder against Sir Gilbert, and he was duly committed to take his trial.

'It was no longer his wife's honour, but his own, that Gilbert had to consider, and he put his counsel in possession of those facts which he had suppressed at the inquest. The trial took place to-day. The theory of the prosecution was this— Discovering her escape from the Abbey, he went at once to the boat-house, knowing that the readiest means of escape was by crossing the river; and there he found Lady Linton in the act of loosening the boat. A violent scene ensued, in which Sir Gilbert, tempted by the opportunity of ridding himself of a wife who had made his life burdensome, or exasperated by her refusal to return with him to the Abbey, thrust her into the water and suffered her to drown, casting the boat adrift afterwards to avert suspicion. The counsel for the defence began by calling witnesses to prove the late Lady Linton's immorality, and the necessity of keeping her a prisoner in order to prevent the recurrence of such affairs as those at Brighton and Scarborough; then witnesses were brought to prove that a secret liaison had for some weeks existed between Lady Linton and John Barton— Sir Gilbert's valet. Other witnesses proved that this Barton was an unscrupulous, reckless rascal, who, while corresponding with his master's wife, was courting that lady's maid, Sophia Kirby. It was proved Sophia Kirby knew perfectly well what was going on between her lover and her mistress, and herself carried the letters that passed from one to the other. She was, in fact, John Barton's accomplice, playing a double game for a high stake.

' A letter was produced which one of the witnesses, engaged as nurse and watch to the lady, had got possession of on the very day of Lady Linton's death. It was from John Barton, fixing the time and place of their meeting. It said :

'" Sir G. has ordered his mare for seven o'clock this evening. Be ready to start if he goes. I shall be in the boat-house, and all ready at eight," or something to that effect.

'It was next proved that, on Sir Gilbert's return from Streetly, whither he had ridden that night, he was informed that Lady Linton had evaded her keepers and was not to be found, and that Sophia Kirby and John Barton were also missing. Evidence also showed that Sir Gilbert's desk had been forced, and his wife's jewels, which he kept there, had been taken. The last witnesses swore that, on the night of the murder, Sophia Kirby and John Barton, both heavily charged with bags, etc., had stopped at

an inn on the London Road, and gone
on the following morning in a hired cart to
the railway-station to catch the first up-
train. The theory based upon this complete
chain of evidence was simple enough.
Sophia Kirby and John Barton had planned
the murder of their mistress—to which the
servant's jealousy would naturally incline
her. They had got the half-witted creature,
closely wrapped in a tight-fitting fur-lined
cloak, into the boat-house, and there
drowned her and made off with her jewels
—a theory borne out by the evidence and
by the fact that, of all the jewels, amounting
to some four or five thousand pounds' worth,
taken from Sir Gilbert's desk, none were
found in the boat-house but the bracelets
and watch which Lady Linton habitually
wore. The prosecution made but a poor
fight after this, as you may suppose. The
judge, in summing up, censured Sir Gilbert

severely for suppressing facts which, in the interest of justice, he ought to have made known; but it was clear that the jury were more favourably disposed towards Sir Gilbert for subjecting himself to the serious consequences of a criminal trial, in preference to revealing a condition of things which threw disgrace not only upon his dead wife, but upon her mother, who was partly responsible for her misdeeds. After a very short absence from the court, they returned with a verdict of " Not Guilty ;" and, thank Heaven, there's an end of it !'

CHAPTER VII.

THE DIARY.—A RIFT IN THE CLOUD.

MAY 3 (Kennington).—Everyone
says to me, 'How well you
look! How bright you are to-
day!' and everyone speaks in a cheerful
tone, and has a great deal to say to me,
and seems sincerely sorry to end the conversation and say good-bye. A little
while ago these same people wore a dejected
air in my presence, found very little to
say, and seemed relieved from an embarrassing position when we parted, which compels
me to think that their sympathy is with

happy people only. Granny alone departs from the general rule. She was gayest and most chatty when she saw I needed cheering, and, now that my spirits are high, she watches me with grave concern and silent anxiety. I am like the trees, I tell her—the spring has given me new life.

' My love,' she replied, ' one must rejoice to see the young buds open, yet timorous old folk like me find their pleasure mingled with the pain of apprehension lest it be found that the young buds have opened too soon.'

I know what she means and what she thinks. She believes that my happiness springs from the expectation, or at least the hope that, now *he* is free, he will make me his wife. I think she is in error. I have analyzed my feelings as well as I can, and tried to form a just conclusion as to the origin of my happiness. For

indeed I am happy—happier than I have
been for a long, long while—troublesomely
happy sometimes, for I find myself growing
careless and frivolous, and too full by
half of nonsense. But I cannot convict
myself of selfishness. If my happiness does
not arise from the improvement in my
physical condition, and the reflection that
he is no longer miserable, I am more in
error than granny. I do not expect him
to marry me. I have learnt during the
winter to see how impossible it would have
been for him to make me his wife, even
had he been free then to marry me. I
know how jealously society maintains the
distinction of classes, how ridiculous romance
appears in actual life, and to what contempt
a man in his position would be exposed
who introduced to people of his own class
an inexperienced girl like me as his wife.
That was shown very clearly in a novel

by a lady—I forget her name—that Beatrice lent me. It was quite a new-fashioned book, with none of the old sentiments in it; and it showed that the best man the authoress could think of married for position, and kept the young lady he really loved as his mistress. And though I do not for a moment believe that Gilbert would have behaved so badly, and that he only suggested my being what he proposed, thinking it would be better for me than to be cast friendless upon the world, yet I can quite understand that, had he been free to make me his real wife, he would have been deterred by the knowledge that society would regard him as a fool. There! Had I any expectation of being his wife— had I any lingering hope that he loved me well enough to propose such a thing, could I write of him in such terms? Could I do him such infinite injustice?

May 4.—I do not know what is the matter with me to-night. I am low-spirited and irritable, and glad to be alone. It's just as they say at Neufbourg: Who laughs in the morning, cries at night. I was ridiculously gay when I found the girls in the parlour on my return from school, and now I'm glad to get away from them. They certainly are regardless of the pain their idle words may give; they might have known that it would grieve me to hear of the change in him—to learn that one so amiable and generous and good had been soured by misfortune, and rendered harsh and cynical and worldly.

It seems that Mr. Gower took Beatrice to Monkden last Sunday—unknown to Mrs. Gower, of course. Sir Gilbert seemed not at all pleased to see them; he was exceedingly polite, very cold and very sarcastic. Beatrice believes that their visit prevented him from going to see some one; she feels sure there must be 'some lady in the case,' because of his dress; she had never seen him so 'correct.' Incidentally they learnt that he was renewing his acquaintance with the people he had 'dropped;' people not of the Gauntly set, but quite the 'upper crust.' Edith thought he must have the intention of going into Parliament by trying to regain his old position in society; then Maud, in her flippant manner, said that in that case he would probably marry some girl whose connections might help him, and wondered whether he would throw the handkerchief to Miss This or Miss That, and was running through a string of names when Beatrice gave her a nudge, with a glance at me, which I happened to catch. Did she think I had any idea of his choosing me, or fancy that I should be sorry to hear of any event which might tend to his happiness or temporal advantage ? Did I not write, only last night, that I had renounced every thought of being his wife ?

*   *   *   *   *

July 1.—Granny, in her sweet gossipy way, was describing Broadstairs to me—whither she had suggested we should go to spend a few days before my holidays were over, ' and pick up a little of the freshness we have lost since the spring '—when the well-known sound of cab-wheels made me turn my eyes towards the road, and start up from my chair as the hansom drew up before the steps.

' It is only Joseph,' said granny, as if she thought by starting up so anxiously I had expected some one of more consequence than he. I don't know whom I did expect, yet certainly my heart fell when Mr. Gower stepped out of the cab ; but not because I dislike him. No one could be kinder to me than he, and, despite his faults, he is a most lovable little gentleman. Perhaps we like him better for his faults, and because we can smile at him. Granny and I look forward to his coming, and always take care to be at home on Monday, for on that day he almost invariably takes tea with us. He never comes without bringing a few flowers or a book for me, and usually he hands a little rush-basket to Jane, containing asparagus, or a lobster, or fruit, or a fine piece of salmon. This being Saturday possibly accounts for my surprise in seeing him ; and, to increase the peculiarity of his visit, he carried neither flowers nor a rush-basket.

' Thanks to the serious illness of Mrs. G.'s brother,' he said, his wife had been compelled to go to Scarborough, and the girls wishing to see the ' Huguenots,' he had taken a box at the opera for this evening. He had come to fetch me. The girls would be at the Holborn Restaurant, where they insisted upon dining, at six o'clock, and, if I would be a good girl and dress quickly, we should be able to get there just in time to meet them.

I looked towards granny, almost hoping she would raise some objection, for somehow I felt no inclination to go out, except for the usual peaceful little stroll with her. But, if she saw the disinclination in my look, she was determined to give me no support.

'Go, by all means, my love. A change will do you good. You are growing melancholy with sitting so much in this dull little parlour.'

So I accepted the invitation with the best grace I could assume, feeling ashamed to make so poor a return for Mr. Gower's kindness, and knowing that I was selfish and ungrateful.

When we were in the cab and on our way to Holborn, Mr. Gower, drawing my arm under his, and giving it one or two little pinches with his, said, in a tone of gentle remonstrance:

'What's the matter with you, little girl —eh? You seem to be going back and back and back, week after week, instead of growing stronger and brighter. You were better in the beginning of the year than you are now, and we all thought you meant to be your old self again a month or so ago. You're much too young, dear, to look so sadly upon life.'

My spirits were so low that his kindness seemed to wring my heart. My eyes filled with tears, despite my endeavours to restrain them, and one went slowly trickling down my cheek. I couldn't say a word;

it was all I could do to keep down a sob.

'Look at me, dear,' he said, pressing my arm to his side again. 'I'm fifty-four. I have had grief enough to break the heart of a cart-horse. I've lost a good wife and married a bad 'ne—I think you'll admit that Mrs. G. is about as bad as they make 'em.'

I couldn't help laughing a little, though the tears fell as I laughed. He repeated,

' As bad as they make 'em, she is. If misfortune could kill a man, I ought to be as dead as that lamp-post. But what do I care for Mrs. G.? Not that!'—with a snap of his fingers. 'And that all comes through treating the miseries of this life as a kind of tax one must pay for enjoying its pleasures. Pay your taxes and be dam to 'em, and get as much fun as you can for your money—that's my principle! Now can't you look at your troubles in the same sort of business-like way ?'

I shook my head.

He shook his also, in mere sympathy, and drew a long sigh as he looked at me.

' No,' said he ; 'I suppose you can't. There's not much resemblance between you and me in any way, worse luck for you ! The girls, you know, take after me. Best girls in the world, but no more capable of fretting for twenty-four hours at a stretch than those sparrows there.'

' It's very stupid, I dare say,' said I : ' but——'

' I don't know about that, my dear. It seems to me that the stupidest people are the happiest. If it were not for the existence of people who take things to heart, the world might be little better than a cage of monkeys. Your light-hearted people die with the echo of their laugh—only deep-

feeling souls are immortal. I fancy I can
see the trace of tears in nearly everything
that's great.' I was surprised to hear the
jovial little gentleman speak so eloquently ;
and he seemed surprised also, and became
silent like a bird that has for the first time
heard his own song. Then presently he
turned to me and asked with a changed
manner : ' Don't you feel sometimes as if
you could be heroic ?'

' I don't remember ever thinking that.'

' I think you might, though.'

I shook my head. ' I only wish to live
a quiet life, like granny's,' I said.

He glanced at me as if in doubt, and
began to whistle softly. But indeed I said
what I felt.

' Well, my dear, I am mistaken, that's
all,' he said, coming to an end of his tune.
' I thought you were still thinking of
Gilbert Linton.'

I felt the blood rush up into my face.   It
did not occur to me to wonder what my
memories of him had to do with the probability of my being heroic.

'Perhaps you don't like to think about
that subject?' he said.

'I don't see why we should not talk
about it, if there is anything to be said,' I
responded, with an eager hope that he
could tell me something.

'Why, that's my opinion, you know,
dear.   I'm for speaking out; granny's for
smothering up everything—as if a wound
were likely to be less painful for not being
seen.   Granny's an old woman.   If anything goes wrong at the bank I just jaw,
jaw, jaw, till there's not another word to be
said, and my experience is that it does good
all round.'

'Yes, but what have you to tell
me?'

' Oh, I didn't say I had anything particular to tell, you know ! Only I thought
that if we talked it over pro and con, it
might set your ideas straight, and give you
some definite notion as to what you ought
to do. If there's no chance of your ever
being Gilbert's wife, you ought to realize
that clearly ; if, on the other hand, you see
a prospect of marriage——'

' Oh no, I don't see that for a moment !
I have no idea of being his wife.'

' No definite idea, I dare say—there's the
result of smothering up the thing so that
you can't see it clearly ! What I say is,
Let's think it over first, and then make
some final decision. After that you will be
able to say, " I've talked this thing out
pro and con. I've looked at it right and
left and top and bottom, and there's not
another view to be taken of it. I shan't
be that man's wife under any condition,

and the best thing I can do is to think of marrying another." '

' Oh no, no, no !'

' My dear, we haven't half talked this matter out yet !'

A long sigh came fluttering up from my heart. It seemed so useless to talk in this way. But I could make no objection to his continuing the subject, which I had encouraged him to discuss; and he continued :

' I say that, if you are assured you cannot marry Gilbert, the best thing you can do is to think of marrying some one else ; for until you do you must feel yourself a kind of martyr, and entertain a morbid and unhealthy sentiment, which it is your moral duty to get rid of. I am sure you are not so silly as to wish to foster useless regrets, or so childish as to pine for an early grave, like a silly girl in a still sillier romance.

You don't see anything noble, or sweet either, in such lackadaisical nonsense as that ?'

I shook my head—albeit I knew that I had given way more than once to the sentiment he condemned, and which I also felt was only fit to be condemned.

'Very well, then, my dear,' he pursued. 'Now we'll proceed to settle beyond the question of doubt that you can't marry Gilbert ; and then we'll consider whether the young Baptist minister, who, I hear from granny, buys more biscuits than should satisfy his hunger, may not be allowed to see you without being compelled to waste his substance in riotous living.'

He referred, of course, to that horrid Mr. Headlam, whose face I hate to see.

'I saw Linton yesterday,' continued Mr. Gower. ' He was in London upon a matter of business ; and, as that business could not

be done without seeing me, he called at
the bank ; otherwise, in all probability, I
shouldn't have seen him, for he's not so
amiable as he was by a long way. Gave
me a nod and kept his hands in his pockets
when we met. Didn't feel like shaking
hands, I suppose. That was not particularly encouraging ; however, as I wanted
to have a few words with him, I managed
to take luncheon with him—very much
against his inclination, I assure you.' Mr.
Gower chuckled inwardly, as if the recollection of the luncheon tickled his lively
vein of humour. ' After luncheon we had
a bottle of claret and cigars—he didn't
seem to relish them either ' — another
chuckle. ' Then I tackled him upon the
subject I had in my mind. I told him how
you had struggled through the winter,
and what a brave fight you had made
of it.'

I made a little exclamation of regret; but he took no notice.

'And then,' he pursued, 'I told him how you had suddenly acquired new life, grown young and gay again, when you found that he was free to make you his wife.'

'Oh!' I exclaimed, snatching my hand from under his arm, and drawing away from him in indignation. He seemed to me perfectly brutal in his indifference to my feelings.

'Very indelicate on my part, wasn't it?' he asked, smiling. 'But that isn't all. I told him how gradually your gaiety died away, and you lapsed into the sad hopeless air of a poor old maid, as week after week passed away and he made no sign of caring whether you were happy or sad, living or dead; and I then asked him if he considered his conduct towards you was consistent with the character of a gentle-

man and a man of honour which he was
trying to establish for himself. That was
pretty plain, wasn't it ?'

I did not answer. It seemed to me
impossible that anyone could dare to
speak in such a manner to him, and most
impossible in such a man as Mr. Gower,
who had not the courage to complain before
his wife when he found his coffee undrink-
able.

' You look as if you thought I risked a
thrashing by putting such a question. I
knew my man, you see ; and, besides that,
I never yet feared speaking my mind to
anyone—of my own sex. Linton didn't
take the cigar out of his mouth. He looked
at me coolly across the table for a minute,
and I expected a sarcasm at the least—
something to the effect that I was not
qualified to judge of what a gentleman's
conduct should be, you know ; but all he

said was, " What conduct would be consistent with that character, Gower?" I
didn't stop to weigh my words, I assure
you, my dear ; but told him plump that he
ought to make you his wife. He replied
that it was impossible. I asked him why
it was impossible. I appealed to his sense
of justice; I told him what a patient,
affectionate, and sweet girl you are. I
waxed quite eloquent, my dear, but all to
no purpose ; he said he couldn't and
wouldn't ask you to be his wife.'

' You had no right to ask him!' I cried
indignantly, my face burning with shame.
' It was an unwarrantable presumption to
think I cared for him; it was an insult to
think I would marry a man induced by
your arguments to make me an offer.'

' It's only natural we should differ in
opinion upon that point, my dear. However that may be, here's the fact. Linton

does not intend to ask you to be his wife;
and, before dismissing the subject, we have
just to consider whether it's possible that
you can ask him to be your husband.'

'We can dismiss the subject without any
such consideration,' I said.

'I don't think we can. You must, first
of all, know what motive he has for not
asking you to be his wife now that he is
free, when he was so anxious for you to
be something of the sort when he was
tied.'

'I do not wish to know anything. You
do not know what you are saying, or you
do not understand that what you say is
repulsive to me.'

'My dear, I know all that. Have a little
patience. You can't get away. I'm not to
be silenced until I've had my say, however
unpleasant it may be. You know that ever
since the trial Linton has been striving

might and main to re-establish his position in society.'

I would not reply or make any sign of listening. I knew well enough that he had been trying to renew acquaintance with the friends he had forsaken. The girls had told me so. And they told me that he would marry, most probably, into some grand family to obtain position. Oh yes, I knew why it was impossible for him to marry me; why he couldn't and wouldn't make me his wife, though probably Mr. Gower did not. It was because he had engaged himself to another. Possibly it was this consciousness that made me bitterly angry with Mr. Gower for trying to force him to marry me.

'He has done his utmost,' continued Mr. Gower. 'For a couple of months he has been trying by every means that a man of his disposition could employ to obtain a footing in society, and overcome the prejudice that exists against him. That astonishes you—eh? You can't understand that prejudice can exist when a man has proved his innocence as clearly as Linton did. You have to consider that the poor devil has Mrs. Gower for an enemy. That indefatigable and vindictive person has circulated a report which society, however distantly removed from her, cannot afford to ignore. Even her enemies cannot deny that there is a grain of possibility in the charge she makes against Linton. There is very little doubt that she herself believes what she asserts; no one can hear her without being impressed that she is acting under honest convictions; and that, together with her untiring zeal in circulating her opinions, does more even than her logic to persuade people that her theory is right.'

'What is her theory?' I asked.

' That Linton, if not the actual murderer
of his wife, was an actual accomplice; that
he was in the conspiracy with Sophie Kirby
and John Barton, and suffered them to de-
camp with his wife's jewels, either as a bribe
or as a sure means of keeping them out of
the country. " Would he have concealed
the facts produced at the trial if he had been
guiltless?" she asks. " Is it possible to con-
ceive that a man, being innocent, could have
acted as he did? Hating his wife and his
stepmother, would he not have taken steps
to separate himself from the one and be
revenged upon the other? Supposing the
story put forward by his counsel at the
time to be true, could anyone give Linton
credit for being in his senses to suffer his
wife and her base-born lover to run off
quietly, taking with them property to the
value of several thousands of pounds?"
People who have no sentiment more delicate

than hers are willing to pooh-pooh the notion of a man being actuated by a nice sense of honour.'

'And people believe her story?' I asked, with a strange feeling of exultation.

'Yes. And unfortunately this attempt of his to get into society seems to strengthen their opinion that he is not blameless.'

'You yourself think that Mrs. Gower's theory is possibly correct?'

'It's a plausible story, my dear—that's all I say.'

'It is not!' I cried. 'There is not an atom of truth in it!'

'Well, my dear, most people think there is. And so they shut their doors in poor Linton's face!'

'Ah!' I exclaimed, my heart bounding with joy, though I knew not why.

'They won't even send their cards in acknowledgment of his visits.'

'Is that true?'

'Gospel. They get out of his way when they see him coming. Servants won't stay in his house for fear of being compromised.'

'Oh, how shameful!'

'And now, thoroughly beaten, or heartily sick of an attempt which must in itself have been distasteful to him from the beginning, he has resolved to be done with it. The Abbey is to be shut up, and, as soon as his arrangements are concluded, he will go away. Probably in a couple of days or so he will leave England, and drop out of sight for ever. That's why I tackled him on the spot, you know; and also, my dear, why I have persevered in talking with you. There's no time to be lost. If he's to be your husband, you'll have to look sharp.'

His language was quite as brutal and indelicate as it had been; but, somehow, since I learnt that Gilbert was rebuffed by his friends, and that his marriage with the daughter of an influential family was out of the question, his suggestion was no longer offensive. But I could not understand what it was I had to 'look sharp' about.

'I suppose you don't see why Linton was so anxious to recover a place in society?' he replied, after regarding me with a quiet smile for a minute or two.

'No,' I answered simply.

'Nor did I at first. And I suppose you cannot imagine why, having failed to obtain recognition as a worthy gentleman, but, on the contrary, having excited a very strong suspicion that he is a villainous murderer, he refuses to console himself by the simple means of making you his wife?'

I felt as if my heart had leapt up from my bosom as I suddenly apprehended the meaning of his suggestion.

' Ah!' I exclaimed. ' He, so proud and strong and independent, has sought to overcome unjust prejudices against him by persistently encountering affronts and patiently enduring insults—all for my sake!'

' I'm perfectly sure he'd do no such thing for his own.'

' And it was because all his efforts had failed to remove suspicion that he refused to ask me to be his wife.'

' That's it, my dear. I'm as certain of it as if he had told me in so many words. At present no one will be seen with him. He's under the ·shadow of a crime, and that shadow would be cast upon any woman he took to be his wife. And so I think I've shown you pretty clearly that there's no hope of his making you an offer, and the

only thing to be settled before we quit the
subject is whether——'

'Where is he now?' I asked eagerly.

'At Monkden.'

'I must go there at once.'

'Oh, nonsense! You're going to the
opera with the girls.'

'Oh no, no, no! I could not endure to
sit inactive for a moment. The last train to
Marlow has not gone yet?'

'Lord, no! there's half a dozen yet! But
don't be unreasonable. You know, my dear,
he's safe to be there to-morrow, and then I
can go with you, and——'

'No; I want no one to go with me, and
I cannot wait until to-morrow.'

'But you won't get there before night-
fall; and just think, you know—you may
compromise yourself by being seen there.'

'What does it matter what people think?
What does it matter what becomes of me,

if I may be his wife and make his life happy?'

'Certainly,' said he, after a little period of silence, 'I have not mistaken the love that dwells behind those sweet eyes of yours.' And then, lifting the trap in the top of the cab, he cried 'Victoria' to the driver.

He tried for some time after the cab had altered its course to dissuade me from going to Monkden that night; but when he at length perceived that it was useless, he ceased to be grave, and joked about my indignant refusal to consider the possibility of overcoming Gilbert's resolution to remain a widower.

I could laugh now, for my heart seemed to have taken wings, and to be bearing me up and up towards the beautiful heaven.

CHAPTER VIII.

THE DIARY.—GERTIE BECOMES LITTLE LADY LINTON.

E had only ten minutes to wait at Victoria. Mr. Gower got my ticket, and put me in the best carriage he could find. Before he closed the door, I gave him both my hands and two good kisses, for so only could I express my gratitude to him. It was a fast train, and yet how slowly it seemed to approach Marlow! I had to walk from Marlow, for I had left my purse at home, and had not a penny in my pocket; but I was glad, for I thought I should get there quicker than if I had taken a dawdling old fly. And indeed I believe I did, for when I was out of the town and on a part of the road where no one could see me, I ran until my breath failed me. 'If I get there too late—if he is gone!' I said to myself again and again; and that prevented my feeling tired.

But he was not gone. The man who came to the door when I rang the bell said, as he looked at me in astonishment, that Sir Gilbert was in the library.

'What name shall I give, miss?' he asked.

'Never mind about that,' I answered. 'Which is the library?'

With some hesitation he crossed the vestibule, and tapped with his knuckles at the door.

'Thank you,' I said; 'that will do;' and at the same time I heard Gilbert's sonorous deep voice say, 'Come in.'

I turned the handle and entered the library; then I closed the door silently behind me, and stood there breathless and unable to move. He was standing by a table covered with books; his back was towards me. A box was beside the table, in which he was putting the books he intended to take away. He had not heard me open and close the door, and he cried again, 'Come in!' as he bent down to put a book in the box. At that moment he caught sight of me, and, starting as though he had seen a ghost, he cried, 'Who's that?'

He caught the lamp from the table and held it up. As the light fell upon my face, he exclaimed:

'God Almighty, Gertie! You again?' And then—'What on earth does it mean?' he asked, coming towards me, for I still stood nerveless by the door.

· I've come to be your wife,' I said.

He thrust the lamp impatiently upon a bracket, and repeated my words in a tone of voice that struck me with terror.

'Don't you love me?' I asked, so faintly that for a moment I thought he had not heard me. He took me by the arm and led me to a seat near the window. The curtains were not drawn; there was yet a faint grey light in the midsummer sky.

'What has that to do with it?' he asked, looking down at me with a sort of wonderment. 'I can't make you my wife, if I love you ever so.'

'Oh, if you love me, Gilbert, you will, for I cannot live without you!' I cried; and then I started up from my seat, for I could not sit there like an unseasonable visitor, while my heart was being wrung with an agony of doubt. I stood trembling before him, like one waiting for the verdict of life or death.

'Gertie, Gertie, do you know what I am? Do you know that even the servants refuse to remain in my service, so strong is the suspicion of crime against me? Do you know——'

'I know all,' I answered. 'If I didn't, do you think I would have come here to ask you to marry me? Do you think I would have been glad to hear that people wouldn't return your visits, and that you could no longer stay among them, if it had not been for the hope that, being quite alone, you would be glad to have me, and that you would love me for being faithful and true to you?'

'Come, you beautiful, divine, sweet soul!' he cried, catching me in his arms, and drawing me close to his breast. 'A thousand scruples—a thousand times more tough than mine—would melt in the warmth of such a love as yours.'

And then he kissed my lips and my cheeks and my forehead and hair with an abandon which showed how great an effort he had previously made to restrain his feelings. Then he began to laugh.

'What?' said he. 'You were glad to hear that I was shouldered out from respectable society, and snubbed all round? How did you learn it? Has the gossip spread so far as Kennington, that I murdered my wife?'

'Mr. Gower told me this afternoon.'

'Ha! I forgive him everything—even to his praises of that young Baptist minister, Mr. What's-his-name.'

'I hate him!' I cried.

'Why, so do I; but I pity him for all that, when I think of what it is to love and not to see you. And you won't go back to that hole in Peckham again?'

'It isn't in Peckham, and it isn't a hole.

I would rather be with granny in Kennington than any place in the world—where you are not.'

He sank into a chair, and drew me down upon his knee, and folded his arms about me. It seemed quite natural to be nursed like that, and very nice. I tore off my hat and let it drop on the floor. My head just reached to the hollow of his shoulder, so that his lips touched my forehead when he turned. We said very little for some time. The moon was rising behind the plantation on the other side of the lawn, and it looked like a great gold shield. A blackbird sang in the distance, an odour of jessamine came through the open window.

'I had no idea the night was so beautiful,' he said in a gentler tone, as though the unexpected beauty had subdued his spirit.

'Oh, everything is beautiful now!' I said.

' Everything has been ugly enough lately,' he said, with a short laugh. ' It was getting more unendurably ugly every day. Gower told you that I was on the point of going away !'

' Yes.'

' Thought of taking a cruise in the *Tub*.'

' Oh !'

' Would you like to cruise in the old boat with me?'

' Yes,' I murmured, nestling a little closer in his arms. It was lovely to lie there and look at the moon slowly rising above the tree-tops that stood out in sharp silhouette against its brightness, and listen to his voice and just say ' Yes ' and ' No,' and think how happy and beautiful it all was.

' After we're married, of course. I suppose his Grace the Archbishop of Canterbury won't keep us waiting long if he gets his fees in full. Would you like to be married

in a church, or would you put up with the
registrar?'

'Don't care which.'

'You'd like granny and the Gower girls
to be present?'

'Oh, yes, yes! They will be so glad!'

'And we'll go away the same day to
Dover, and the next morning, quite early,
steer the *Tub* over the waves, like a good
old tub as she is.'

'Mpse.'

'Sail over the old course, Gertie, pass
the island, and away over the Channel to
Noailles.'

'Yes.'

'I've wanted to make that voyage again,
but hadn't the heart to make it alone.'

'Poor dear!'

He was silent. Indeed, I know not how
the time passed. The moon had risen
above the trees, the blackbird had gone

farther away, so that his song sounded no louder than an echo. The scent of roses, I thought, was now mingled with the perfume of jessamine. He passed his fingers gently over my head, so that the caressing touch was just perceptible. When he spoke again, his low voice sounded like a lullaby of which my drowsy senses caught the tone, but not the meaning; a feeling of sweet repose lulled all my senses, and in this calm, succeeding the fatigue and excitement of the evening, I fell asleep.

The moon was far above the trees when I awoke; it seemed not more than half the size it was when my eyes last saw it. I was still in his arms.

'Do you feel better for your sleep, Gertie?' he asked.

'Yes. I must have been asleep for a long time. Haven't I moved?'

'Only once—to put your arm about my neck. Don't you remember?'

'No;' and yet I must have been sufficiently conscious to know that he was there, and that it was his neck I wished to caress.

The next day we went to London. Our first visit was to an office near St. Paul's, where Gilbert arranged about the license of marriage. He saw the look of astonishment with which I looked at the little dry old clerk and the bare walls; and, laughing, said :

'I suppose you expected a temple hung with roses, and a cupid in place of that very ordinary old tax-collector.'

Then we had luncheon, and he made me think of everything that I should be likely to want for six months, and wrote all down ; and when the list was made and luncheon finished, we drove off in a cab to Regent Street, to buy the things. We went from one end to the other, looking in all the shops; and it was dinner-time before I had bought all that I needed, so quickly did the time pass—in my calculation. I cannot enumerate all the things that Gilbert bought in addition to those I actually wanted; and indeed I think I must skip over a great deal of happiness, or I shall not finish my task of bringing up my diary to date before he comes in to dinner.

We were married at Kennington Church, and as there had been no time to make a grand wedding-dress, I wore the costume we had bought in Regent Street, and which the young lady there had taken in very nicely. It fitted me beautifully, and everyone said I couldn't look nicer in anything. Gilbert bought me a lovely bouquet. He wore his grey suit, with just two buds

in his button-hole that I had taken out
of my bouquet. Granny was there, looking
like a dear old picture ; she cried a little
when no one was looking at her. Mr.
Gower gave me away ; he looked the most
stately and ceremonious person in the
church, after the pew-opener ; and his collar
was so particularly stiff that he could
scarcely turn his head on his fat little
throat. The girls were my bridesmaids,
and they cried a little ; but they did not
suffer very much, for they rejoiced sincerely
in my happiness, and, moreover, Gilbert
had given each of them a diamond ring
which they could not keep their eyes away
from. We had luncheon at the Cannon
Street Hotel, and were very gay—almost
too gay, in fact, for Mr. Gower, who was
in a serious humour and wished to make
a speech. Whenever he got on his legs,
posing his knuckles on the table and

leaning forward with a solemn air, the girls began their nonsense, and continued it until, unable to do more than open his mouth like a fish for the continual interruption, he was himself at length tickled by the ludicrous situation, and sat down with a chuckling laugh. Then he would drink a glass of champagne, and rise again, more serious than ever, and one would ask him if he felt better, another beg him not to laugh, or the third cry ' Hear hear !' before a word was spoken. Granny was greatly scandalized at first, saying that it was right and proper to make speeches on such an occasion as this, and it was in very bad taste, to say the least of it, to prevent their papa saying what doubtless he had taken a great deal of pains to compose. However, she herself finished by joining in the irreverent laughter when Mr. Gower, for the sixth time, put his knuckles on the table, and leant forward with his mouth open. A coupé was reserved for Gilbert and me, and when the time came, we took our places in it. Then, when everyone was rather silent, not knowing exactly what to say, Beatrice, with a sudden sparkle of gaiety in her eyes, approached the window, and said, with mock respect:

'We shall hope to receive a letter soon from little Lady Linton.'

The other girls caught up at once the alliterative title, and, as the train moved away, they cried together:

'A happy journey, little Lady Linton!'

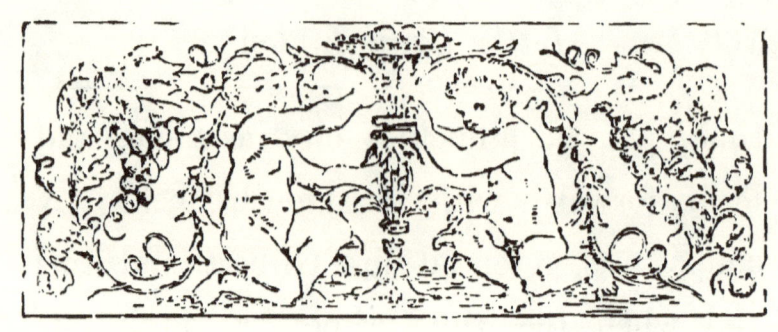

CHAPTER IX.

CORRESPONDENCE.

Letter from Mr. Pierce, London, to Mrs. Pierce, chez Sir Gilbert Linton, Valvins, Fontainebleau.

'Pierce and Pierce, Private Inquiry Agents,
'Endell Street, Long Acre, London,
'*June* 16, 188—.

'DEAR ELIZA,
        'Your packet, bringing the copy of Lady Linton's diary up to the date of her marriage, to hand this morning—and precious little of it! For Heaven's sake, send more, and with fewer intervals—there's a dear good soul! In all,

there were only twenty-two pages last
week. Mrs. Gower comes every morning.
For three days I had nothing to give her;
what she got in the other three was hardly
worth having. There's a dry parched look
about her face, as though she were con-
sumed with a thirst for discovery; these
exasperating driblets are enough to drive
her out of her mind. She was sallow to
begin with; she looks almost green at
times now. And no wonder! Just think
what she's had to put up with since she
began this precious inquiry. She has
learnt that her husband and his children,
and even her own daughter, are all leagued
together to deceive her and expose her
to the ridicule and mockery of their friends
—that Mr. G. is in constant and friendly
communication with her avowed enemies—
the old rascal was absolutely tender with
Miss Graham, you know, after her dismissal

from the position she held ; that he and
her children bribe the servants to deceive
her, turn the house out of the windows
in her absence, and spend money lavishly
on pleasure in which she takes no part ;
and, knowing all this, she has to hold
her tongue, and so to conceal her emotions
that her family may continue their rioting
without suspecting discovery. Upon my
life, I can't tell what motive you had
for sending all this irrelative matter!
From the first and throughout I have been
expecting—and so has Mrs. G.—that the
diary was going to show us Miss Graham
implicated with Sir Gilbert in the murder
of his wife. On the contrary, she seems
to be a remarkably decent sort of girl,
so far as I can judge, and Sir Gilbert
is not half such a bad lot as I expected.
It must be mortifying in the extreme
to Mrs. G. to make this discovery. Of

course the diary only represents one side
of Sir Gilbert's character—that which
appeared to the enamoured eyes of a young
girl—and I suppose you have found out
a lot to his disadvantage. Even in his
wife's description there are passages which
show pretty clearly that he meditated
putting his wife out of the way at the
time he was making love to her. I
wish, Eliza, if you have any damning
fact against him, you would let me know
it. It would be so gratifying to Mrs.
G. Without that, I fear there must soon
be an explosion—she can't hold in much
longer ; and, whether the row takes place
at Gauntly House or in this office, the
result is likely to be disastrous to our
plans. She couldn't have endured in
silence so long if she hadn't the malignity
of the very devil in her heart. And, even
with that and the hope of one day getting

full revenge for all she has suffered, it is a marvel to me how she tolerates the present condition of things. Fancy a famished wretch hunting barefoot over a stubble-field for scanty ears, which must be threshed and ground before anything can be got to satisfy her cravings—her feet lacerated at every step, her search resulting in nothing but the finding of empty husks, and her hunger continually increasing, and then you can understand what that poor devil of a Mrs. G. has to suffer. This sort of thing has been going on for a couple of months. We've drawn a cheque from her for fifty pounds; and what on earth has she got for it? Nothing but the satisfaction of seeing herself as her enemies see her. I don't like the woman a little bit; but I can't help feeling that we are taking an undue advantage of our position, and I can tell

you candidly, Eliza, that if I hadn't been
held by your hints of ultimate success,
and by the constant anticipation of something turning up to prove the guilt of
the parties we are supposed to be acting
against, I should have given up the business
before now, and looked about for some
other employment more congenial to my
tastes and abilities.

'My position is deucedly unpleasant. I
feel like an impostor every time I see our
client, and I'm sure I look like one. She
is such a shrewd woman that I couldn't
deceive her, even if I had the hardihood to
try. She knows I am a living fraud, and
no more fit to be a private inquiry agent
than the man in the moon. At first I used
to sit up at the desk and pretend to be
busy writing when I expected her; but her
steely grey eyes seemed to run through
me, and the curve in her lips said as plainly

as words, " You know that's all a sham,
and so do I." Now I sit in my chair—
which suits my frame considerably better
than that tall rickety stool—and when I
hear her step outside, I just drop my newspaper and perspire, wondering what on
earth I shall say if she demands an explanation of our movements. She hasn't
expostulated yet a while—perhaps she
knows it's no good doing so—and will
mark her perfect contempt for me by
remaining silent. Upon my word, I think
it would be a relief if she kicked up a row
and refused to continue the affair.

' This leads me, Eliza, to the question I
had in my mind when I determined to
write to you and set the state of affairs
clearly before you. Don't you think, my
dear, that we had better retire from this
business? You must have read the diary
through before you began to copy it, and I

conclude there is no direct evidence of Sir
Gilbert's guilt in it, or we should have had
it long ago, instead of this history of Miss
Graham's griefs and joys, which has nothing
whatever to do with it.   Of course, as there
are pretty nearly eleven months of the diary
yet to be copied, the inquiry can be dragged
out until the end of our term of agreement
with Mrs. G.; but it doesn't seem to me a
fair way of getting money, and it most
certainly isn't a pleasant one for me. 'If
you have nothing more satisfactory to send
than that we have already had, I strongly
advise—indeed, I think I must insist upon
coming to some arrangement with Mrs. G.,
and winding up the affair.   In yesterday's
Telegraph there was the advertisement of a
roadside inn in Hampshire, with a skittle-
alley and a long garden, for sale, and that
would just suit me.   I dare say we could
raise the money somehow to buy it; and, if

the thing only brought us in bread-and-cheese, it would be better than carrying on this business, which is a source of continual worry and self-reproach to me. Let me know what you think at once, my dear, and believe me,

'Affectionately yours,

'JOE PIERCE.'

From Mrs. Pierce, Fontainebleau, to Mr. Pierce, London.

'Fontainebleau, *June* 18.

'DEAR P.,

'For gracious' sake, get that roadside public-house out of your head at once. I knew before I had read the first half-dozen lines of your letter that you had got hold of some new idea. It is a repetition of the folly which has kept us in constant poverty and anxiety since the day we were married. How many schemes, I wonder, have you tried and abandoned for others equally disastrous, or more so ? It's the Paracelsus cigarette agency and the market-garden all over again exactly. Just when you were beginning to think of buying a dogcart to travel with the cigarettes, and I was looking forward to a little peace, you gave up the agency and took that wretched piece of waste land at Tottenham, and all because some person found out that the cigarettes were not filled with genuine tobacco—as if their name wasn't sufficient to have told you that at first. I tell you plainly that I shall not live in any roadside public-house in Hampshire. I am not an old woman, and decline to be buried alive in a desert. I can't for my life understand what possesses you!

'Your size and temperament unfit you for any occupation requiring energy, and you have said over and over again that the most agreeable exercise you know of is reading the newspaper in a comfortable armchair. This agency — which is in a fair way to become most remunerative— provides for your requirements, and, I may add, for mine also. You can sit and read your newspaper the whole day ; I will do all the work. With no family and no inclination for domestic pursuits, and with a natural ability which you have frequently commented on for what you term "ferreting out" the secrets of other people's affairs, the agency provides me with an occupation which is exciting, useful, and remunerative, and which I could not relinquish without a regret that would be lifelong, and the cause of unceasing reproaches which you would have to bear. Do be reasonable, Joseph, and let me assure you at once that your most absurd objections are without the slightest foundation. You must have faith in me; so must Mrs. G. I know what I'm about, and, if you leave the management of this affair in my hands, the result will satisfy all your scruples. I am sure that, before the six months have expired, I shall have evidence to convict Sir Gilbert. If I don't tell you all I know, it is because I believe the facts are safer in my keeping. You can no more keep a secret than you can fly in the air; and if Mrs. G. knew what I know, she would interfere, and all would be lost. It is most unmanly of you to fear Mrs. G., and most irrational at the same time. In the first place, we have her agreement, and, whatever she thinks of us, she is bound to sustain the investigation. As I said before, the result will clear you from any suspicion of unfairness, and at the same time establish our reputation for sagacity and address.

'There is nothing to fear from Mrs. G. The regularity with which she calls at the office for information proves how eager she is to continue the inquiry. If you offered to throw up the affair, she would insist upon your going on; and that you are bound, by every consideration of justice and honour, to do. You need be under no apprehension of her betraying the knowledge she has obtained to her family, for she must see that such an act of folly would prevent her obtaining more; nor need you fear any scene in the office. In your last letter you told me that she had divined that your wife was the active partner in the firm of Pierce and Pierce; knowing that, she will have the greater faith in the ultimate success of our inquiry. There is not one man in a thousand could do what I am doing—I say this not from vanity, but from a conviction that women are eminently superior to men in occupations of this kind. This Mrs. G. knows as well as I do. Should she take advantage of your obvious feebleness to demand an explanation of our plans, two courses are open to you—you can quietly decline to tell her anything at the present stage of affairs, or you may justify all that has been done and all that we are doing at present. I should most certainly take the first course ; but, as your temperament is very different from mine, and you will probably prefer the latter, I will reply to the objection you make in your letter, in order that you may be prepared to meet any that Mrs. G. may trouble you with. In the first place, you find fault with the small quantity of information I send, and the long intervals which sometimes occur between one budget and the next. Ask Mrs. G. if she expects us to purloin the diary entire, and what good she thinks it would do our cause if we consented to such an act of dishonesty. If she agrees that it is advisable to get a copy of the diary, she must also admit that we must do so with caution.

'If I were discovered making extracts from the journal, or even examining it, there would be an end to the affair. In the first case, I should be dismissed summarily; in the second, the book would be removed to a more secure place, where I could not get at it. I can only copy in the absence of Lady Linton. There are days when she does not leave the house, and others when I have to refrain from taking advantage of her absence, in order to avoid the suspicion of servants. As I play the part of confidential lady's-maid, the servants of course hate me; and if they saw that, whenever Lady Linton was out, I locked myself in my room, they would find means

to discover what it is I do there at those
times. You seem to think Mrs. G. is
justified in feeling aggrieved because the
extracts from the diary do not prove Lady
Linton guilty of complicity with Sir Gilbert
in the murder of his first wife. Isn't that
expecting almost too much of a private
inquiry agent, Lady Linton being innocent?
You say that all we have produced is
irrelative to the inquiry we are making. I
deny it. We have proved that Sir Gilbert
had a stronger motive for getting rid of his
wife than mere dislike to her, and, had the
Court which tried him for murder possessed
our knowledge, it is exceedingly doubtful
that he would have been acquitted. To
understand Sir Gilbert's character and the
motives with which he acted, his acquaintance with Miss Graham and his relations
with her must be fully explained, and I
maintain that not a line I have sent could

have been omitted without weakening the evidence against him.

' Another advantage has been obtained by these extracts—they have shown Mrs. G. the absolute necessity of keeping her proceedings secret from her husband and the daughter she trusted ; and still another —of the greatest importance to me—it has sustained her interest while I have been securing my position here and forming my plans for the future guidance of this affair. My object is not only to prove that Sir Gilbert did put away, or help to put away, his wife, but to obtain such evidence as will enable us to convict him of it and bring him to justice ; and this I do not doubt of obtaining, if time and perfect freedom of action are granted me. For your greater satisfaction, I will inform you that the extracts from the diary which are now to come bear directly upon Sir Gilbert's crime, and that before long you will have evidence which shall fortify even your faltering spirit.

'Now, Pierce, I am going to give you some instructions, which I beg you to carry out to the best of your ability. You will tell Mrs. Gower that your partner has given you inquiries to make which will necessitate your leaving London for eight or ten days. What these inquiries are you must decline to tell her—and mind you don't tell her, or she will attempt to help you and do more harm than good. You will go to Monkden, and there find out all that you possibly can find relative to Sophie Kirby. Don't go about it as if you were a police-constable. Take your fishing-rod with you, and be content to spend the days by the side of the river, talking to anyone you chance to meet, and getting, if possible, some information regarding Sir

Gilbert and his family without exciting suspicion. In the evening you will go to an inn — choose one where the village people meet, if possible—and there you will make yourself agreeable to anyone who talks, and do your best to *find out facts concerning Sophie Kirby.* But do not let it be seen that you wish to know; if you can't lead up the conversation to that subject easily and to your own satisfaction, abandon it for the time, and talk about your fishing or any other topic you like. But if you bear in mind that you want to learn something about this woman, you are pretty sure to find some means of acquiring facts. Stay away from London just as long as is necessary—that will relieve you greatly from your apprehensions of Mrs. G.'s attack—and let me know anything you learn. I will send the next packet to " J. P., Post-office, Marlow," and, when you have read it, you will post it to Mrs. G. at any address she likes to give.

'Lady Linton has rung for me, and I have no more to say.

'Affectionately yours,

'E. PIERCE.

'P.S.—I hope this will show you the folly of turning your thoughts to any other occupation.'

CHAPTER X.

E dined at an hotel quite close
to the beach; and, oh, how
delicious the look and the sound
and the smell of the sea were to my senses!
A great many boats lay in the harbour;
but I distinguished at once the dear old
boat that had brought me from Normandy,
and pointed it out to my husband.

'Ah, we shall have to re-christen her,
Gertie!' said he. 'The *Tub* was good
enough for Diogenes; but now that Diogenes is an altered man——'

'It shall keep its old name all the same, if only to warn you from falling again into the folly of thinking like Diogenes,' I replied.

Then we laughed and talked nonsense—at least, I did—and we were exceedingly happy.

After dinner we walked upon the pier, and I was so excited with pride that my feet seemed scarcely to touch the earth ; for my husband was the finest man of all the fine men who were there, and everybody looked at him with admiration ; and when I said to myself, ' They can see I am his wife,' I felt that I, too, was more to be envied than any of the grand ladies. My husband—oh, it makes tears of pride and joy come into my eyes to repeat those words, ' my husband '!—looked to my eyes handsomer than ever I had seen him ; and, being happy, he held up his noble head, not with his former look of defiance, but rather with an air of exultation—it was the difference, I thought, between a soldier going out to the battle and him who returns triumphant.

It was just such a morning as I hoped for the night before, when we left Dover— such a day as that on which I first saw the sea, and had since recalled to mind so frequently as the most memorably beautiful. There was the same clear atmosphere, the same white luminous clouds scattered over the blue sky, the same vigorous breeze that filled the sails and carried us with joyous bounds over the nimble waters. All was sparkling and gay and beautiful and quick ; and it did one good to breathe deeply the salt air. It was like some grand strain of music, that makes one think how beautiful it is to live. As I stood, holding my dear husband's arm, it seemed to me that the sea and sky promised us a future of happiness as pure and boundless as theirs ; and I told him this, for I was full of courage, and my heart could have no secret from him, no pleasant thought that I would not have him share. He pressed my arm to his side, and then, his smile turning to a laugh, he said :

'Peter says there's bad weather brewing.'

Peter is the old seaman who had been so kind to Mère Lucas, and he had come to the hotel the night before to pay his ' respectful dooty' to my ladyship, and to inform Gilbert that the orders he had telegraphed were executed, and that the *Tub* was ready to put to sea.

I should have but very little to write about our voyage, one moment being as happy as the other, but for a chain of circumstances that seemed to give my husband

great displeasure, and which consequently
troubled me. It was when we came upon
deck after luncheon that I first saw a look
of annoyance upon my husband's face ; he
was looking over the sea in our rear.

'What is the matter, dear ?' I asked.
'Is the storm Peter foretold gathering ?'

'Oh, I don't care a straw for Peter's
omen !' he answered.

'Then what annoys you ?'

'I don't know that I'm annoyed yet.
Do you see that sail out there ?'

'The ship with two masts ?'

'That's it. Well, she has followed us
ever since we started. When we shook out
our canvas, she shook out hers, and she
has kept in our track and at the same distance all the morning.'

'Perhaps she can't help it ?'

'Oh, she could have passed us and gone
out of sight by now, if she chose !'

'Maybe her captain is not so bold as you are, and is afraid to go too quick,' said I.

He laughed.

'Of course it may be purely accidental,' he said. 'On the other hand, it mayn't.'

'What purpose could anyone have in following us ?'

'The purpose which impels a fool to make himself unpleasant. The owners of yachts are not all gentlemen ; a linendraper may keep one if he likes; that sort of person, having a very feeble sort of wit, finds pleasure in giving annoyance, like stupid boys who break windows or ring bells.'

I knew that there were such people, for many times when I was going from granny's to Miss Fletcher's, and even when I was walking out with granny in the evening, young men who looked like linendrapers had followed me for no possible reason but to make me uncomfortable.

'However,' added Gilbert, 'we will soon see whether we are followed by accident or design!' And then he called Peter, and gave him some directions as to the management of the ship. Soon afterwards the shadow of the sail fell upon the other side of the deck, and I perceived that we were taking a new course. We sailed on for half an hour, and then it became clear that the strange yacht was following us intentionally, for it stood apparently at the same distance in our track, as my husband pointed out to me with gloomy anger.

'If they see we take no notice of them, dear,' said I, remembering what granny used to say with regard to the young men, 'they may perhaps grow weary of following us.'

He nodded. But again he had the course

altered, watching the result with evident anxiety. The yacht followed us still.

I did my best to divert his attention from the thing which annoyed him, and so far succeeded that he did not again refer to the subject; but more than once I saw his brows bend as he looked over the waters at our pursuer.

Towards night the clouds thickened, and the wind grew stronger.

'We can run into shelter, if you like, Gertie; but if you are not afraid, and don't mind a shaking, we'll keep out,' said my husband; and he glanced towards the ship behind us.

I told him I had no fear, and should prefer to keep out; and so, when it grew dark, he put me in my hammock, tucked me up, and, kissing me sweetly, said good-night. Then he went on deck, and I was alone.

It was a terrible night; the ship gave such lurches that I trembled lest my dear husband should be thrown from the deck. Sometimes a wave struck the side and burst with a fearful noise over my head, and all the boards and beams creaked with the strain. Many times he came down to see me, his oilskin suit glittering with wet in the light of the swinging lamp, and it gave me great joy to see that he was safe ; but I kept my eyes closed, that he might not be concerned on my account. Nevertheless, I was very much afraid, and never lost consciousness in sleep until a faint grey light appeared through the little round window, and the comparative stillness showed me that we had come into smooth water. Then, when my dear came down, I kept my eyes open and held out my arms, and drew his darling face down and kissed it again and again, and again.

'We're in harbour now, sweet,' said he, 'and I'm about to turn in. Close your eyes again.'

And so I did, and soon fell asleep with a happy heart.

It was late when I got up. Breakfast was waiting in the cabin, and I found my husband reading a book.

'Have we got away from our enemy?' I asked, when at length I got up from his knee and we proceeded to seat ourselves at the table.

'Not a bit of it!' he replied, with an impatient laugh. 'She's lying not a hundred yards off.'

'Of course you have said nothing?'

'Oh no! That would be too gratifying to them.'

'I don't see why we should mind what stupid people do, while we are free to do as we like.'

'That's the philosophic way of looking at it; but unfortunately we can't always conform with logic. Peter says we are to have fine weather now; that's cheering.'

After breakfast I went up, and with some curiosity looked at the yacht which had chased us so persistently. There was nothing remarkable in its appearance. It was longer and more elegant than our boat, and had two masts instead of one. A man was lounging against the side with a pipe in his mouth. He didn't look like a linendraper, so I supposed that he was one of the crew. That he was there to watch us was evident, for no sooner did our men begin to carry out Gilbert's order to leave the harbour than he quitted his place and called out to the people down below. Directly afterwards five or six men came on deck and set to work; and we had not passed the head of the pier five minutes before our enemy did the same. And she followed us steadily, just as on the day before. Once, when my husband had left me, I took up the glass he had left, to see if I could distinguish anyone on deck. To my astonishment, I perceived that the scarlet speck which had excited my curiosity was a woman's jersey, and that the wearer was also looking through a glass. Just then my husband came upon deck.

'Gilbert, dear,' said I, 'there is a woman on that boat.'

He must have already found that out, for he was not surprised.

'Does that astonish you, Gertie?' he asked. 'I thought you had learnt that women can be as objectionable as men. Don't bother your little head about the confounded thing!' said he, taking the glass from me.

And thenceforth it was he who sought

to make me forget the 'enemy'—as I accustomed myself to calling, in my mind, the pursuing yacht, and when I looked about for the glass later in the day, I could not find it.

It seems to me now that I was absurdly agitated by the senseless persecution of these stupid and vulgar people. This was no more than a practical joke, and, unpleasant for the most part as practical jokes are, sensible people, one thinks, should not suffer more than irritation from them. But indeed there was something almost terrible in being constantly pursued — to know that if you turned your head you would see the following ship just where you had last seen it; that as we flew before the wind in the darkness she was flying behind us; that if we changed our course she would change hers; that when we stopped she too would stop. It seemed almost as though our enemy was an enemy indeed, and had some fell motive in tracking us. It was the cause of a kind of reciprocal discomfort between my husband and me. He saw that I was uneasy, and that made him more concerned, and seeing that increased my uneasiness, so that it seemed as if our distress grew out of each other. A source of absolute distress it eventually became to both of us, and when, having put in at Cherbourg, my husband said to me, 'Take Peter with you, Gertie, into the town, and purchase the things I have put down in this list,' I felt sure that he intended to board the yacht, which, as usual, had anchored quite close to us, and remonstrate with the people on board.

I went into the town, and purposely lengthened my errands. Gilbert was walking on the quay when I returned.

He said nothing concerning what had happened in my absence, and I dared not question him, for I saw that there was no change in his manner, unless it were that he was more uncomfortable than ever. The only reference he made to the subject was on the following morning, when he gave Peter his orders.

'We will run round to St. Malo,' he said. 'If we don't shake off this bugbear by running, we must slip away by stratagem.'

The enemy followed us to St. Malo.

CHAPTER XI.

THE DIARY.—HOW THE ENEMY WAS CHEATED.

IT was a lovely morning when we left Cherbourg. A light breeze favoured us, and the motion of the sea was not too great to allow of our sitting on the deck or moving about with ease. After a glance behind us had assured him that we were still followed, my husband set our chairs to face the bow of our boat, and seated himself with a sombre expression of determination in his face, as though he had resolved to look at the yacht and think of it no more. He was unhappy, I could

see that. It was with difficulty that he
found matter for conversation. For my
part, I felt so grieved to think that he
suffered, and so perplexed to understand
why he took the annoyance so deeply to
heart, that I was even more silent than he.
It was a great relief when he proposed that
I should read to him.

'Anything will do. It doesn't matter
what words go to the music of your voice,'
he said; he put his hand in his pocket
and drew out a volume. 'Ah, here's the
"Autocrat." That's pleasant reading at all
times.'

I read. I knew that his eyes were upon
me, and that made me happy. I don't
think I gave much attention to the matter;
my only care was to look out for the marks
of punctuation. Now and then I looked
up and encountered the soft sweet gleam of
his gentle eyes; when I had found my place

again and subdued the fluttering in my
heart, I continued. I was holding the book
in my right hand, and he took my left hand
from my lap and held it in his. That made
me stop again, and, seeing happiness and
love in his dear face, the tears started to my
eyes, such joy was in my heart to think I
was a comfort to him. I held out my hand
to be kissed, and, after a tender little embrace, I composed my feelings as well as I
could and went on again. He still held my
hand, and I continued reading, though my
left arm ached with holding the book so
long in one position. I wouldn't for the
world take my hand from his, though I
perceived after a while that his thoughts
strayed from me, and he perhaps was unconscious that he held it. My arm seemed
to hang like a heavy leaden weight from
my shoulder; there was a piercing sensation
in my wrist and fingers, and this was fol-

lowed by a numbness, while the pain in my
shoulder grew so intolerable that at length
I was forced to alter my position so that I
could have the book on my knees and read
it. He did not notice my movement, but
still held my hand. And now I continued
for a long while, and did not pause until my
back ached and my head grew dizzy with
being bent down. Then I had to change
my position again.

‘Go on, Gertie, unless you are tired,’ he
said. ‘You can’t tell how sweet your
voice is.’

That gave me new strength, and I forgot
all about my stupid little aches and pains.
It was only the sound of my voice he heard,
for, when I asked him to translate a line of
Greek that brought me to a stand, he
turned abruptly, as if he had been woke
from a sleep, and asked me what it was I
said.

It was time for dinner when we reached
St. Malo. I had read, with very few pauses,
since luncheon, and neither of us had ever
looked at the ship behind us ; yet I feel
sure it had been in his thoughts, and I
know it had occupied my mind far more
than the 'Autocrat at the Breakfast-
table.'

What had taken place during my expe-
dition through the town of Cherbourg? My
fears took a rather absurd form, yet not an
unnatural one, perhaps. I dreaded lest my
husband in his interview with the people on
board the yacht had lost his temper and
challenged some one to fight. I could only
by this wild supposition explain his distress.
I thought that possibly he was wondering
what would become of me if he fell. I
know now that it was excessively stupid to
imagine such a possibility. When I came
upon deck, after changing my dress, I found

my husband standing with his arms folded
and his chin upon his breast, looking at
the yacht our enemy, which was stationed
so near that I could almost distinguish
the features of the men who were moving
upon it.

'What is it, darling?' I said, slipping my
hand under his arm.

'Ah! You there, Gertie?' he said,
turning to me. He took my two hands
in his, held me at a little distance from him,
looking at me with great love. 'Have
I ever seen you in that dress before?' he
asked.

'Yes, two or three times.'

'Then it is you who improve, and not
your dress, for I never saw you look so
pretty before'—and he drew me to him,
and lifted me off my feet in his embrace.
'What should I do without you, my love?'
he murmured.

'And what should I do without you?' I echoed.

'Ah,' said he, putting me down and moving towards the side of the ship, his arm about my waist, 'that is a question! What do you think would become of you without me?'

I detected, or thought I detected, a serious thought under the pleasantry, and at once my imagination flew to that absurd possibility of an impending duel. It seemed to me that he was still calculating upon the chance of being separated from me for ever. I could not move—a tremor seized me—I looked up at him in speechless terror.

'Why, Gertie,' he exclaimed, catching me closer with his strong arms, 'do you think I had a serious meaning in the question?'

'Tell me you had not, dear,' I said.

'You sweet soul! Would I let anything

on earth part us, now that I have made you mine?'

'Tell me that—only tell me that!'

'I will now, if you like.'

'You will let nothing tempt you to—to —to jeopardize your life?'

'Why, what do you mean, you poor fluttering dove?'

'You are not going to fight anyone?'

'Now you puzzle me more than ever. What can you be thinking about, Gertie?'

'You—you went to see the linendraper last night, while I was in the town, and I thought perhaps——'

He burst into a loud laugh, and happily there was no need for me to finish my faltering sentence.

'You're right in one respect,' he said, when he ceased to laugh. 'I did go on board that cursed boat last night; but there was no linendraper to fight—more's the pity, perhaps. But how came you to think of such an unlikely thing?'

'It seemed to me that you were thinking to-day what would become of me if—if——' I could not continue.

He looked at me with wondering gravity.

'Good Heaven! Who would suspect you had it in you?' he said, in a low tone, that was not addressed to my ear; then, with a changed voice and a lighter air, he added: 'Appease your troubled spirit, sweet! I shall not fight, and no power that is shall separate us in this world.' He kissed me passionately again and again, and I clung to him in the utmost happiness that any soul can feel.

I suppose there was no one upon deck or near enough to see us, or he would not have taken me in his arms at first; yet, had all the world been looking on, I should have been unconscious of them, all my faculties being so completely centred upon him I loved.

He led me up and down the deck—I had regained my strength—and as we walked he spoke.

' I have been upset, and made uneasy a good deal, Gertie, I admit,' he said. ' Perhaps my depression results from too much happiness, perhaps the state of my digestion makes me morbidly sensitive. Whatever the cause may be, the fact is that the confounded yacht over there, following us about in this insane fashion, worries me beyond endurance. The sea makes me superstitious; it has that effect upon many men, you know.'

' Then why should we stay on the sea if it causes you to be unhappy?' I asked.

' That's just what I was thinking of talking to you about, dear. I thought that perhaps if we went to Paris for a week, I might shake off this stupid feeling.'

He spoke with embarrassment—not at all in his usual manner, but as if he were ashamed to acknowledge his own weakness and his yielding to it.

' We will start this very moment,' I said.

' I wish you would raise some objection, Gertie, so that I might play the hero by overcoming my own inclination, or the tyrant by overcoming yours, or any part rather than this of a sneaking coward.'

' Oh, Gilbert !'

He regarded me with a strange expression in his face ; I could not tell whether he pitied or admired me.

' Tell me,' said he, ' that you have grown tired of the sea, and that you would be highly delighted to abandon the plan we made for a cruise of six weeks.'

He must have read my thoughts, for

indeed what he bade me tell him was in
my mind. But I feared now to say so, lest
he should think me a fool to change so
quickly.

'Tell me,' he continued harshly, 'that
you would rather by half dwell in a noisy
city than drift along the sunny coast.'

'The sweetest place in all the world is
where I see you happy,' I said.

The harshness was no longer in his face
when he spoke again, but only the expression of love unalloyed.

'What a big soul you have, little sweet-
heart!' said he. 'Will you always love me
so fully, I wonder?'

I nodded with confidence and joy, and
kissed his shoulder, which was near my
lips.

We were gay at dinner; he talked about
Paris, which seemed to be not at all a
murky city from his description, and I

became quite eager to see the Champs
Elysées and the Boulevards, and the wonderful shops.

'When shall we start ?' I asked.

'To-night, if we succeed in shaking off
the enemy.'

'I had better pack up my things directly
after dinner, then.'

'Oh no ; a valise would betray us ! We
have to make our escape, you know. What
is indispensable you must put on your
back, or I will put it in my pocket. The
rest can be bought in Paris. By-the-bye,
have you any strong affection for that
dress ?'

'No.'

'Good ! Now look up another that you
like better to take with you. I shall want
you to change your dress when we get on
shore, and let me have that you wear now.
That astonishes you, Gertie—eh ?' he asked,

laughing at my perplexity. 'Ah, you have yet to see the subtle side of my character !'

'Shall I have to change my hat as well?' I asked.

'Yes. I didn't think of that. If you can find a veil, so much the better.' I did as he desired; and he put the dress and hat I had selected in the canvas bag which Peter used to fetch stores from the shore; then, when I had finished all my preparations for departure, we left the dear old ship in the small boat, Peter rowing us to the land.

It was still light, and, before we reached the shore, I perceived that a small boat had put off from the enemy. The distance between us was great, yet I fancied that I could see a woman's figure in the boat. Gilbert saw the boat also, and, as we landed, he said :

'Go to the big hotel over there, Gertie ;

Peter shall accompany you. I will be with you in a little while.'

He then walked away to that point which 'the enemy's' boat was making for, while I, with an uneasy feeling of apprehension, went, attended by Peter, to the hotel. It was some time before Gilbert arrived. It was no longer light; the lamps were lit in the street.

'Have you changed your dress, Gertie?' he asked.

'Yes; here are the things.'

'Good. We shall want them presently.'

He thrust his hands into his pockets, went to the window, and looked down into the courtyard of the hotel. He took no notice of me. Suddenly he drew in his head, and said, in a tone of relief:

'Ah, here they are!'

Then he went to the door and held it open. Shortly afterwards, Peter came

into the room, followed by Hutchins, the
man who served as servant on board the
Tub, and Joe, the cook's boy, both on
the broad grin. Peter carried a bundle
under his arm.

'Here are the things,' said my husband,
pointing to my dress ; 'take them into the
next room. Come with me, Gertie.'

We went down to the salle-à-manger.
Gilbert bade the garçon bring some Chart-
reuse and the bill. His silence and obvious
inquietude frightened me.

'It's nearly all over,' he said, in a
reassuring tone, as he pressed my hand.

He paid the garçon—giving him rather
more for himself than the note amounted
to ; then we went upstairs again. There
was a good deal of giggling and suppressed
laughter audible as we drew near the
room ; and, on opening the door, I perceived,
to my utter amazement, Peter arranging

my bonnet on the head of a young woman,
and a gentleman with a beard like my
husband's helping with his advice ; but,
as I soon found, the lady was only the
cook's boy Joe in my dress, and the
gentleman was Hutchins in my husband's
jacket, with a false beard—which, as I
was told afterwards, they had had much
difficulty in finding. It was laughable
to see Joe take Hutchins's arm and lean
towards him, as I suppose he had often
seen me do, and the men seemed to think
it was a fine joke. Only Gilbert looked
angry and stern.

'Oblige me by remembering that I
am here,' he said. 'Come, Peter, look
sharp !'

There was no more tittering after that.
Peter stuffed Hutchins's and Joe's jackets
in the canvas bag, and, having touched his
little black ringlet to us, went downstairs.

Two minutes afterwards, Hutchins, with
Joe on his arm, followed.

My husband had thrown himself into
a chair with his back to the men, and
sat in gloomy silence. When they were
gone, I went to him and put my hand
on his shoulder, and said :

'They are gone—it's all right now,
dear !'

'Thank God !' he murmured, drawing
me down on his knee and kissing me.
We waited only a few minutes ; then he
lifted me, and rose to his feet.

'Come along, Gertie ; we'll go and
see if the dodge has succeeded. If it has,
we'll breathe again; and to-morrow we'll
fête our escape with the best luncheon we
can get in Paris.'

At that moment the garçon opened
the door, and, seeing us, stopped short
in bewilderment. Then, with stuttering

apologies, he explained that he thought he had seen us leave the hotel five minutes ago.

'Tant mieux,' said Gilbert.

CHAPTER XII.

THE DIARY.—LITTLE LADY LINTON'S NEW HOME.

E went down to the quay; it was deserted. The night seemed less dark there than in the town, where the gas was lit. A faint grey light like a mist hung over the sea; the anchored boats near at hand looked like flickering shadows as they rocked to and fro on the waves. Farther away were a few lights slowly moving—they were fishing-boats going out with the tide, Gilbert told me. He could see more clearly than I could,

and he understood the position of the
quays, the rocks, and the landing-places,
which so bewildered me that I could not
recognise even the place where we had
landed a couple of hours before. We walked
along the quay to a point where it turned
at an angle, and there were a few yards
of iron rail set up as a protection. There
we stopped, and, leaning on the rail, looked
over the waters in silence. I knew that
he could distinguish among the distant
lights those of our ship, though I could
not, and I shared the anxiety I was sure
he felt, and my eyes went from one light
to another, eager to detect the first movement. For quite a quarter of an hour
we watched them ; then—

'One is moving, is it not, dear?' I
whispered.

' Yes,' he answered, nodding. ' You can
bid the *Tub* farewell ; now for the other.'

We were silent again. The lights of our boat moved farther and farther away, and still the others remained stationary. A fear lest the ruse had failed began to creep over my mind, and I watched more strenuously than before.

'Ah!' Gilbert exclaimed suddenly, in a tone of relief. 'Do you see, Gertie?'

I hesitated a moment; then I felt sure, and pointed to another double light that was moving from its position.

'That's it. The enemy is gone, and a pretty voyage Peter is likely to lead her. Now for Paris, my Gertie, and a cloudless continuation of our honey-moon.'

Saying that, he caught me up in his arms and kissed me with an access of gaiety which showed how greatly his heart was relieved.

'Yes,' said he, turning to take a last

glance at the lights, 'they're fairly off,' and all we have to do is to forget them.'

Then we turned our backs on the sea, and walked across the port to the Grande Rue. On our way he said, after a little silence :

'You've asked scarcely any questions about the " enemy," Gertie, though I dare say the subject has been pretty constantly in your mind lately. If there is anything you'd like to know, anything you'd like to have explained, you know—better have it out at once, so that we may talk it to death, and bury it for ever.'

'I think you would have told me anything you wished me to know, and I want to know no more than that,' said I ; and so, with one accord, we despatched the subject from our thoughts — or at least from our conversation—and have not once referred to it since.

We stayed in Paris ten days, and I think we went everywhere and saw everything; at any rate, on the tenth evening I. hoped so. On that evening, as we sat outside a café by the Madeleine, we counted twenty-four van-loads of Cook's tourists, returning from Versailles, pass by; and then Gilbert said:

'I think there'd be enough of our com-patriots in Paris without us, don't you, Gertie?'

'Oh yes!'

'Would you like to go to Fontaine-bleau?'

'Very much, if—if there isn't too much to see.'

'Oh, hang the palace! I'm thinking of the forest. It would be a pleasant change to see a few respectable trees.'

'Lovely!'

'Then we'll start to-morrow.'

I gave his hand a little pinch without being seen, to let him know how pleased I was.

The next day we left Paris and went to Thomery, which is the second station beyond Fontainebleau—quite in the heart of the forest, with not a house near ; and, oh, how delightful it was to breathe the pure air and walk in the chequered shade of the great trees, holding my dear husband's hand, without any fear of being seen ! The country reminded me a little of some parts of Neufbourg, only that the trees were much finer, and the paths were not encumbered with great rocks, but beautifully kept and quite pleasant to walk along ; and, after we had walked some distance, we came to a hill covered with gardens, each with a long wall covered with vines, and at the foot lay a village bordering the river, from which upon the other side rose a great hill covered with oaks and firs, and broken here and there by a crag of grey rock. It did us good to see the water again, and indeed I do not know who could regard without delight the beautiful broad river sweeping in a majestic course between the noble wooded hills, and presenting a perfect crescent to the eye.

We followed the course of the river, keeping close to the water, yet under the pleasant shade of the trees ; and when we were tired we sat down, and Gilbert smoked a pipe while I arranged a bouquet with the wild flowers we had plucked on the way.

' Jupiter, there's a fine jack !' said Gilbert ; and he pointed through the reeds to a big fish with a long nose that lay perfectly still amongst the stems of some lily-leaves. ' And look at the roach out

there! They look as if they'd never seen
such a thing as a rod and a line. One
might be very lazy and very happy here, I
should think.'

I agreed with him; that was only natural,
his suggestion being so pleasant.

'With a boat for the river—an English
boat, Gertie, not one of those barges we
saw at Thomery—a comfortable house with
just a glimpse of the water, and enough
ground about it to support a cow and some
poultry, so that we could laugh at the
irregularity of the local butcher, and
stabling for a pony-chaise and a cob or
two——'

I didn't at that time know what cobs
were; but the picture he drew was so
enchanting without them, that I let my
bouquet fall in my lap, and could think of
nothing but the pleasure of living in such
a place.

'Go on, dear,' I said, when he stopped.

'Well,' said he, laughing, 'I can think of nothing to add to the attraction of such a dwelling, except a graceful little lady, daintily-dressed, piquante in the matter of silk stockings and Louis Quinze shoes'—I drew my feet under me—'to welcome a fellow on his return from a day's fishing. Do you like the picture, lady?'

'Oh, it's ten thousand times better than that Lake of Como picture!' I said. 'And when you had changed your clothes and got rid of your fish, dinner should be served — served as well as it could be served, with flowers on the table, and the wine you like quite ready, and the linen and glass as white and bright as possible; and a fire burning on the hearth when the evenings grow cold—not a cinder fire, such as they have in London, but bright blazing logs, clean and sweet-smelling. And I might have some chickens and little ducks.'

'Oh yes,' said he; 'the only difficulty is where we are to put our little ducks!' and he looked up at the hills despairingly.

There was one château in sight, but that seemed to me much too large and fine for our requirements; besides which, it was clearly not to let—and there was no other house in sight.

'After all,' said I, with a sigh, 'there's no harm in supposing.'

'Not a bit. It would be more delightful, though, to realize our dream. Here comes a fellow with a hotte on his back; I'll tackle him on the subject. If I mix my tenses very unintelligibly, come to my assistance, Gertie.'

When the peasant came up, Gilbert

spoke to him, and at once went to the point by asking if he knew of a house to let. The peasant shook his head. One must go to Fontainebleau for a house, he said ; there were not enough in the country for those who had to work in the fields ; and, if one was to let, it was snapped up at once, despite the rents which were so high—ah, so dear—so dear that one could with difficulty find anything nice at two hundred francs a year !

' Two hundred francs a year won't do for us,' said Gilbert. ' What's " haunted château " in French, Gertie ? Ask him if there isn't anything of that sort to be had; an old farm-house would do.'

I explained to the peasant, who had set down his hotte and seemed well disposed to enter into the affair, the kind of house that would suit us ; and he, after describing a number of residences that we could not

have, and which would certainly not suit
us if we could, suddenly recollected that
there was a house within a kilomètre which
was just our affair. It was not a farm-
house, to be sure, nor was it old ; but it
had grounds about it where a dozen cows
might be kept, and the garden abutted
upon the very path we were pursuing. It
had been bought, decorated, and furnished
last spring by a Parisian, who failed in
business in the summer and had been compelled to sell it in the autumn ; and
Madame Masson of Valvins kept the keys.
We had only to follow the path for three
kilomètres, and on our way we should see
the ' bonbonnière,' and be able to determine
whether we should like to live in it.

To my eyes the house was charming,
standing in the midst of a beautiful garden,
with a smooth green lawn sloping up to
the great bay-window that occupies nearly

the whole of one side, and a hill behind it
covered with fir-trees, and nothing to inter-
cept the splendid view of the river and the
hills opposite but a line of poplars.

I looked up at my husband's face, to see
if he liked it as well as I did.

'Gas, Gertie!' said he, in a tone of
objection.

There was a handsomely gilt lamp on each
side of the perron at the front of the house.

'We need not light it, dear,' said I.

'That's true; and I suppose the lamps
could be rooted up. The silver globes on
the lawn might also be got rid of; then the
place would seem less like a casino, and a
little more like a habitable home. The
grounds stretch a good long way apparently
—plenty of room for your little ducks, and
flights of steps along there for them to
come down to the river when they're
thirsty.'

'That would be convenient when we wanted to go to the boat—and, see, dear! there's another flight of steps from the path down to the water. You wouldn't have to go far to fish, would you?'

'Not if the ducks were reasonably quiet. You seem to like the look of it.'

'Oh, I think it's lovely! Up there under the veranda is just the place where I should sit and look out when it was time for you to come home, and through the open windows behind I fancy you could see the silver and glass sparkling on the table. Wouldn't that be nice if you felt hungry?'

'Gertie, we'll have that house, if money can buy it.'

Then we hurried away in search of Madame Masson, with my heart quite in a flutter, lest we should find that the house was not to be had.

But it was to let; and Madame Masson

said the proprietor would be only too glad
to find a purchaser who would take the
furniture as well as the house. And she
went with us and showed us all the rooms,
throwing back the persiennes that we might
see the beautiful view outside, and the
elegance and luxury of the apartments
within. It seemed all too exquisite for
me—the furniture and apartments surpassed
in beauty anything I had ever seen or
imagined. It fairly bewilders me to think
of the painting and gilding, the plush and
velvet and lace, the marqueterie and ebony,
the pictures and statuettes and consoles,
crowded with lovely little knickknacks;
the carpets and furs and beautifully par-
quetted floors, and the portières and lovely
little screens to the fire-place; and then
the quantity of linen neatly stored in
armoires, and crystal and porcelaine, and
the arrangements for warming the vestibule

and staircases. While Madame Masson was showing me the kitchens, Gilbert strolled away to explore another part of the house.

'There's a very good den at the back, with a capital billiard-table,' said he, when he returned.

'There's everything, I think,' said I.

'And you think it will do?'

'If it isn't more than we ought to have.'

'More than you ought to have, Gertie! Do you consider gold too good for the gem that is set in it?'

*   *   *   *   *

And now he has gone to Paris with the notary from Fontainebleau to conclude the purchase of the beautiful house which is to be our home. He went this morning, leaving me in this little house at Valvins. I have been writing nearly the whole day, and my fingers ache; otherwise I think I could find yet more to tell of the happy days which have passed since I left dear old Mrs. Simpson at Kennington.

CHAPTER XIII.

CORRESPONDENCE.—PIERCE AND PIERCE ON THE TRACK.

From Mr. Pierce, Monkden, to Mrs. Pierce, Fontainebleau.

'The Swan Inn, near Monkden, Berks,
'June 26.

'DEAR ELIZA,

'I followed your instructions with the utmost promptitude—starting for Marlow by the 4.35 on the day I received your long and most satisfactory letter. I locked up the office, and left a note with the housekeeper, to be given to Mrs. Gower when she called the next morning, thus avoiding a meeting with the lady and the cross-examination to which she would surely have subjected me. You can't tell how much easier I felt in my mind after reading your ample explanation. I quite agree with all you say, and have not once thought of the roadside inn since reading your express dislike to the notion. I took my fishing-tackle, as you suggested—though where you put my fly-book when you turned out my cupboard in the spring I could not discover—and arrived at Marlow without accident, though I nearly lost my top-joint in jumping out of the carriage. I went at once to Monkden, determined to lose no time in making inquiries, and found this inn, which is very comfortable, and not over-dear. After a meat-tea, I had a chat with the host, who is a first-rate fisherman, and I arranged with him to bait

over-night a run which seems to swarm
with fine roach. I thought about Sophia
Kirby, as you desired, but somehow the
conversation didn't get beyond fishing. I
had glorious sport the next day, but regret
to say found no one to talk to upon the
subject of the Linton murder. In the
evening there was a very agreeable sort
of free-and-easy in the parlour; but the
singing did not allow me to broach the
subject of S. K. I sang " The Heart bowed
down," " Hot Codlings," and " The Death
of Nelson," and was encored for each one.
So far, I am sorry to say, my inquiry was
fruitless.

'The next day I nearly caught one of the
finest perch I ever saw. Friday, thirty-two
dace. Saturday, not much, but a chub
weighing nine and three-quarter ounces,
and the best I ever tasted. I did not
neglect business, my dear, although en-

joying myself uncommonly, as you may
suppose from the fact that last night—
Saturday—when I observed in a casual
way that it wasn't such a day as this
on which Sir Gilbert Linton's wife was
drowned, one of the customers cried,
"Why, gov'nor, you seem t' got that
there murder on your brain!" Perceiving
that I must be more guarded in my
approaches, and being anxious to send you
a good report of progress, I went for a walk
this evening instead of going to church,
and succeeded in making a discovery which
I think you will admit reflects credit on my
ingenuity and perseverance.

Coming to an inn — the "Chub and
Float," if I remember rightly, which lies
on the farther side of Monkden, about
a mile below the Abbey—I found five or
six village worthies seated in the arbour,
and smoking. I called for a clay pipe and

some ale, and fell into conversation with a fellow in his shirt-sleeves, who evidently knew everyone there. A showy young woman brought the ale that I called for. As she went away I looked after her with a kind of puzzled look, and said I to my new acquaintance:

' "Dear me, it's odd!"

' " What's odd?" inquired he.

' " Why, I seem to know the look of that young woman's face!" said I.

' " That's not unlikely," said he, " if you've been in the habit of visiting these parts."

' " Ah, to be sure!" said I. " Now I know. I must have seen her at the Abbey."

' " The devil you have! When?"

' " Oh, some time ago! Her name's Sophia Kirby, isn't it ?"

' " No. that it ain't," said he. " And

I'm not particularly obliged to you for finding any likeness between the two, seeing as that's my wife, and Sophy Kirby's about as for'ard a hussey as ever lived."

'This rather took me aback, for I had no notion the man was the innkeeper, or the young woman his wife; however, I did not lose my presence of mind, but made the best apologies I could, and assured him that, when I was at the Abbey, a good time ago, I had heard Sir Gilbert speak in high terms of his mistress's maid.

'" No offence, I hope," said I.

'" Oh, none where none is meant!" he replied, shaking my hand. " What you say about Sir Gilbert's praising of Sophy is like enough, seeing as she was something more to him than a maid."

'" How's that ?"

' " Better ask your friend Sir Gilbert," said he drily.

' " Oh, Sir Gilbert's no friend of mine!" said I. " I only went to the Abbey for a few days to look into some accounts which had got into a muddle. It struck me that the master seemed to be on pretty friendly terms with the young woman—that's how I came to notice her."

' " Friendly terms—ah, I should say they was!"

' " Why, you don't mean to say that his wife's maid was——"

' " She was, though, according to all accounts," he said, nodding his head significantly. " I ain't afeard of speaking now, because it ain't likely as the Baronet'll ever show his face again in these parts; and, if so be I hadn't been afeard of losing my license—which a landlord can never be too partic'lar—I might have spoke afore to a pretty tune. I suppose you know there were a murder up there?'

' " A murder!" said I, looking thunderstruck.

' He put aside his glass to make room for his elbow on the table, and, leaning towards me, went over the history of Lady Linton's disappearance and the subsequent investigation and trial, very much as we know it.

' " The jury acquitted of him and let him off," he said, in conclusion; " but, if I'd been on the jury, they might have starved me to death before ever I'd a-jined in that verdict —perviding I wasn't afraid of losing my license, you understand."

' " Why, how's that ? The evidence seemed to clear him, at all events."

' " Yes, and I dur say if you see a angler going home with the grass poking out of his basket you'd think it was full o' fish,

wouldn't you? I know better 'an that.
What's evidence but so much grass as can
be got for the pulling, and just serves to
hide the hollow truth and gull the public?
I tell you, sir, that Sophy Kirby was the
mistress of that house. Not a servant in
the place could contrary her. The housekeeper wouldn't stay in the house with her.
It was her as had that poor ill Lady Linton
locked up as if she was a lunatic or a thief
—it was her who domineered over everybody. And why did Sir Gilbert permit her
to domineer over everyone and maltreat
his wife? Because, sir, she was his hussey.
This was the house of call for his gardener,
his hostler, and his butler, and they all told
me the same story. Now, sir, tell me this
—Why did Sir Gilbert say nothing of the
disappearance of Sophy Kirby and Barton
at the time of his wife's disappearance, when
people were dragging the river for the body,

and his mother-in-law, who suspected the truth from the very first, was letting all the world know her suspicions of this murder? Why, sir, it was to give Sophy Kirby time to get out of the country with the jewels that were Lady Linton's private property, and establish herself before the facts came out! I tell you for a truth, Sir Gilbert and that woman together did the murder, and it was all a schemed job from beginning to end, and everyone in the county knows it. He stayed till it got too warm for him, and then he bolted; and now he's living in Canady with Sophy Kirby."

' " How do you know that ?" I asked.

' " From a gent who saw 'em there only the week afore last."

' I hinted that the gentleman must have travelled with great speed.

' " Be that as it may," he retorted, " it

stands to reason they're together some'eres.
It ain't likely that a woman like Sophy
Kirby would let such a catch as Sir Gilbert
slip when she'd got him on her line.   If he
didn't go to her of his own free will, which
it is likely enough he did, seeing as absence
makes the heart grow fonder, as the song
says—she could make him come to her by
threatening to go to him."

' " She couldn't do that without risking
apprehension."

' " There's no saying what a woman won't
risk to get at a man as she thinks is trying
to get away from her—not as I allow that
he did try to get away from her.   But any
way, you may lay your life on this, sir—
there ain't a woman in the world of that
sort who would let a man as had been her
lover and her accomplice in guilt slip out of
her hands while there was anything to be
wrung out of him; and whether they're in

Canady or elsewhere don't matter a jack-straw—they're together some'eres."

'A man taking a seat at our table put an end to our conversation, which I have set down as exactly as I can. You will see, Eliza, that the innkeeper's tale agrees in many respects with our suspicions, and with certain events revealed in the extracts from Lady Linton's diary which you have forwarded during the week. It quite alters the aspect of the case, and I am happy to think that our inquiry is likely to result in a discovery which must justify your expectations and raise us to an honourable position. Unless you write to the contrary, I shall continue my inquiries here, and see if anything of further importance is to be pumped out of the man at the "Club and Float." I have sent your enclosures to Mrs. G., who must be thoroughly satisfied now, not only with the quantity of matter

you have sent lately, but with the conclusive nature of the information it contains. Hoping that you are in good
health, and that the weather with you is as
fine as with us,

'I am your affectionate husband,

'Jos. Pierce.'

*From Mrs. Pierce, Fontainebleau, to Mr.
Pierce, Marlow.*

'Valvins, Fontainebleau, *June* 29.

'Dear Pierce,

'The information you have obtained
may be useful. By all means continue
your inquiries at Monkden. We must
not be hampered by any interference from
Mrs. G., and the less you see of her at
this time the better. If she writes, asking
for information, reply, as briefly and in as
business-like a style as possible, that at
the present stage of the inquiry our pro-

ceedings cannot be made known even to her—success being dependent upon absolute secrecy. Obtain all the information that is to be had relative to Sophia Kirby and the position she held at Monkden Abbey, but be careful not to arouse suspicion by being over-anxious. We must know more about John Barton, whose part in the tragedy seems to be ignored. When you have heard a statement, discover to the best of your ability whether the person from whom you had it is trustworthy or a liar. I shall not trouble myself to make any more extracts from Lady Linton's diary at present, which, from the date of her arrival here in July last up to the present moment, contains nothing but the account of everyday doings that are perfectly unimportant to us. Sir Gilbert and his wife have hardly any acquaintances here—the châteaux are empty until the end of the

Paris season, and the rest of the world are
of a very common kind. Sir Gilbert
goes out occasionally, and has brought
a few men to dinner; but they seem awed
by the magnificence and luxury of the
house, which they had little reason to
expect from the unpretentious simple
manners of Sir G. Occasionally Sir G.
and Lady L. go to Paris for the opera or a
play, leaving here one day and returning
the next. They are as perfectly happy
together as any two people can be. Sir G.
loves his wife passionately—and more than
that. This is not surprising, for little
Lady Linton is the most sweet and beautiful young woman I ever encountered, and
quite the lady. Her whole thought seems
to be of him, and every action is shaped
with a view to his happiness. And yet she
is not slavish in her love—if you understand what I mean. She has her own

opinions, and very strong and clear ones they are too, of right and wrong; and I am sure she would not go from her principles even to please her husband; but she has no reason to oppose him, for he, either by her leading or out of his great love for her, always sees things in the same light as she. But I can see that, happy as they are together, there is anxiety at the bottom of their hearts—a fear on his part which he dares not reveal—a depression in her mind which she could not explain. His love is greater than is natural even in a good husband for a good wife—and we know why. I have seen an expression on his face exactly like that which poor Tom had when the doctor told him Charlotte couldn't live a week. Don't you remember? He knows that, if that woman finds him, there will be an end of his wife's happiness and his.

'Lady L. detects the terrible anxiety that underlies his happiness, and, without knowing the cause of it, is troubled.

'All this, Joe, shows that we are on the right scent.

'As I said, the diary of the last eleven months contains nothing but a description of happy days, of trips on the river, of rambles in the forest, of visits to Paris, and the beautiful presents he makes her. Their happiness is further increased by the fact that Lady L. is going to be a mother before long. If I send any extracts it will be merely to keep Mrs. G. quiet.

'Now, Joe, the time has come for action. The first thing is to prove whether the woman on the yacht which pursued Sir Gilbert and his lady from Dover to St. Malo is Sophia Kirby or not. There is no doubt in my mind that it was she, and that in the interview Sir Gilbert had at

Cherbourg she refused to accept his bribes. The diary shows us that John Barton knew of Sir G.'s attachment to Miss Graham. For his own purpose, he would excite Sophia Kirby's jealousy. If John Barton were in love with her, he would naturally be piqued by her love for his master. Possibly he was in communication with one of the servants at the Abbey, and heard of Miss Graham's visit to Sir G. He knew all about Sir Gilbert's yacht, and indirectly learnt through Peter of his intention to make a cruise. All the facts point to the conclusion that the woman seen on board the pursuing yacht was Sophia Kirby. Sir G. contrived to throw her off the scent; we shall see what happens when we put her once more upon his track.

'Put the following advertisement in the *Times, Daily News, Telegraph,* and any other paper you think likely to fall into the hands of S. K. or John Barton—*Lloyd's* might be as good as any for such people as they :

"SOPHIA KIRBY.—If Sophia Kirby, lately in the service of Sir Gilbert Linton, will communicate with A. B., care of Mrs. Binks, 4, King's Square, Goswell Road, she will hear of something greatly to her advantage."

'Aunt Mary will receive and send on to you any letter that comes, if you ask her. If S. K. does answer the advertisement, send the letter under cover to me at once, and I will instruct you how to act.

'Yours affectionately,

'E. PIERCE.'

CHAPTER XIV.

CORRESPONDENCE.—MR. PIERCE RETIRES FROM THE BUSINESS.

From Mr. Pierce, Monkden, to Mrs. Pierce, Fontainebleau.

'The Swan, *Tuesday.*

'DEAR ELIZA,

'I haven't inserted the advertisement, and I don't mean to. I don't like the business, and I shan't go on with it. There's a candle-manufactory at Marlow to be disposed of, and, though it is not a pleasant trade in warm weather, I'd rather devote my energies to that than to ruining the happiness of two unfortunate people by this confounded private inquiry. You must have a heart as hard as Lady Macbeth's to look upon the abounding love of sweet little Lady L. and the yearning affection of her husband, and calmly lay your plans for blasting their lives and making them miserable for ever. I'd forgive Bluebeard himself if he showed for his last wife such earnest and tender feelings as you ascribe to Sir G. I *do* remember that expression upon poor Tom's face when he heard that he had only a week more to look upon his dear girl's face and hear her voice ; and if Sir G. has such an expression as that, then my heart's with him, and confusion to his enemies ! say I.

'You will do me the kindness, Eliza, to come home as soon as you can, and let me know how we are to manage with Mrs. G. I don't suppose she will expect us to give her the fifty back ; but it will be as well to retire from the business as decently as we can. Anyway, if we have to give her the fifty pounds, there will still be enough, if we sell out of the building society and raffle the piano, to get the candle-factory, which I am told will be worth double the money when the hot months are over. I think you had better write to Mrs. G. You can tell her that my inquiries here have not yielded those results we expected; and this you can do truthfully. I find that the landlord of the "Chub and Float" is one of the greatest liars in Berkshire—which is saying a good deal, especially in this part of it, where a man never lands a gudgeon without swearing he's caught a bream. The stories he has told me about barbel-catching prove how little his word is to be relied on. I have found nothing reliable to add to what I told you in my last ; and, as that was false, you may safely write to Mrs. G. that further inquiry is useless.

'I shall wait here until I receive your answer to this, and then return to town. have in the broker from the bottom of Endell Street to re-purchase the office-furniture, and close the show.

'Yours affectionately,

'Jos. Pierce.'

From Mrs. Pierce, Fontainebleau, to Mr. Pierce, Monkden.

'Valvins, *July* 2.

' Dear P.,

'If you are not quite a fool you will have nothing to do with the candle-manufactory. You will live in it alone if you do take it. I defy you to raffle the piano. It is legally mine. You are

welcome to do whatever else you please—
close the office, sell the desk and the
rest, and welcome. I can conduct the
business better, perhaps, without you. One
thing is certain : I shall not defraud our
client by retiring from an undertaking to
which we are solemnly pledged by an
inland revenue stamp. I have sent the
advertisement with a mandat de poste to
the London papers, and I have written
to Mrs. Gower. Irrespective of my feelings,
you will see the necessity of doing nothing
to make Sir G. acquainted with the inquiry
I am making. If you speak, you will
oblige me to give Lady L. an explanation
of my conduct. Your letter containing
the account of a conversation with your
friend of the "Chub and Float" will
suffice. The only chance of happiness
Sir Gilbert and his wife have is in my
failure and Lady L.'s ignorance of this

inquiry. I have no wish to "b—t their lives," as you profanely put it. I only desire to see justice done and provide the means of subsistence for ourselves, which your energies, devote them as you will, have hitherto failed to procure.

'Yours,

'E. Pierce.

'P.S.—You need not trouble yourself to call upon Aunt Mary. I have written to her, and she will forward to me whatever is sent there in answer to the advertisement.'

From Y. Z., Post Office, Southampton, to A. B., care of Mrs. Binks, King's Square.

'July 8.

'To A. B.,

'I am instructed, on behalf of Sophia Kirby, to inquire what advantage is referred to by the advertisement which appeared in the *Times* of yesterday, May 14. Please communicate in the first instance with

'Y. Z., Post Office, Southampton.

From A. B., London, to Y. Z., South-ampton.

'July 10.

'To Y. Z.,

'A reward of one hundred pounds will be paid to Sophia Kirby if she furnishes within ten days such evidence concerning the murder of the late Lady Linton as shall lead to the conviction of Sir Gilbert Linton, now residing at Valvins, near Fontainebleau, France. A personal interview with Sophia Kirby is desired, and she is requested to appoint time and place for a strictly private meeting.

'A. B.'

From Mrs. Pierce, Fontainebleau, to Mrs. Gower, London.

'Valvins, Fontainebleau, *July* 10.

'DEAR MADAM,

'My partner in London, Mr. J. Pierce, being wholly occupied in procuring evidence concerning the relations which existed between Sir Gilbert Linton and Sophia Kirby antecedent to the date of the late Lady Linton's death, I take upon myself the duty of acquainting you with the progress we are making in the commission with which you have honoured us. We have obtained, not without considerable risk and difficulty, a copy of the diary kept by the present Lady Linton—formerly Miss Graham—which gives evidence (1) that she is guiltless of any complicity in the murder of the late Lady Linton—a most important fact, which precludes the disastrous consequences of wrongly accusing a person whose innocence could be proved to our confusion; (2) that Sir Gilbert Linton was passionately enamoured of her while his first wife was alive; (3) that he offered to abandon his wife for Miss Graham's sake; (4) that, after her refusal, he meditated getting rid of his wife as the only means of realizing his desires with regard to Miss Graham; (5) that, after getting rid of his wife, he did not at once go to Miss Graham and repeat the offer he had previously urged so passionately, which was the natural course for an innocent man to take; (6) that it was with a desperate disregard to consequences that he at length resolved to marry Miss Graham; (7) that, to escape those consequences, he proposed to leave England and lead a roving life—the best calculated to avoid a meeting with his accomplice,

Sophia Kirby; (8) that he recognised at once an enemy in the yacht that pursued him from Dover; (9) that the woman seen upon the pursuing yacht was neither to be bribed nor frightened from her pursuit, as shown by her persistence in following Sir Gilbert after the interview he obtained with her at Cherbourg; and that (10) she was to be feared, and at all hazards to be prevented from encountering his wife, clearly demonstrated by the ignominious ruse practised at St. Malo, the flight to Paris, and subsequent residence in an obscure village on the Seine. These facts led us at once to the conclusion that the woman so strenuously avoided was Sophia Kirby, and that she was not wholly guilty of the murder; for, had Sir Gilbert been guiltless, he would beyond doubt have handed her over to the police instead of making his escape from her. Our next

efforts were to discover the exact relation
which existed between Sir Gilbert Linton
and Sophia Kirby prior to the murder.
We succeeded in finding that she was his
mistress, and that their connection extended
back to a date earlier than that of Sir
Gilbert's first meeting with Miss Graham.
Mr. J. Pierce is at the present moment
prosecuting this branch of the inquiry with
unrelaxed energy, and we may confidently
hope to obtain further and conclusive
evidence before long. At the same time.
we have been seeking Sophia Kirby; and I
am happy to inform you that we are now
in direct communication with her.

'It is contrary to our principles to
disclose the proceedings we intend to take;
but confidence in your complete secrecy
and discretion permits me to indicate the
course we intend to pursue in this case.
We shall intimate to Sophia Kirby the

hiding-place of Sir Gilbert; if our conclusions are just, she will avail herself of this information to seek him at once here at Valvins. The result of their meeting may be the immediate denunciation of Sir Gilbert, or a secret compromise. In either case the conviction of Sir Gilbert is inevitable; though in the latter it may be for a time postponed. Rest assured, madam, that I shall acquaint myself with all the particulars which can contribute to a satisfactory conclusion of our inquiry, and that I shall not neglect to apprise you of the facts as they occur.

' Believe me, madam,

' Yours respectfully and obediently,

' E. PIERCE.

' P.S.—Kindly address all communications to E. Pierce, poste restante, Vulaines sur Seine, Seine et Marne.'

From Mrs. Gower, London, to Mrs. Pierce,
Fontainebleau.

'Gauntly House, *July* 12.

'Mrs. Gower writes to express her entire satisfaction with the manner in which Messrs. Pierce and Pierce have conducted their inquiries on her behalf, and also her confidence in their integrity and business ability. Mrs. Gower encloses a cheque for the amount due to Messrs. Pierce and Pierce to present date.'

END OF VOL. II.

BILLING AND SONS, PRINTERS, GUILDFORD.
G., C. & Co.